Praise for Music Notes...

A terrific legal thriller that draws you into two cutthroat worlds--law and the music industry. Filled with great characters, well-researched law, and suspenseful mysteries, Music Notes kept me turning pages long into the night!

—Larry A. Winters,
Jessie Black Legal Thrillers

When the first paragraph of author Manning Wolfe's novel, Music Notes makes you smile in anticipation, and the succeeding paragraphs build on it to create a razor sharp legal thriller filled with characters so lifelike they could be your friends, well, you know you've got a winner on your hands. An excellent novel by a truly gifted author. Buy it, you can't go wrong.

—Billy Kring,
Hunter Kincaid Mystery Series

With Merit Bridges and her Austin based staff, Manning Wolfe gives you some lawyers you can love. This time a case puts Merit through a byzantine plot that weaves its way through the town's colorful music scene. She describes the city with such vibrancy and passion, as a local I'm happy she kills off a few people to discourage more Yankees from moving out here.

—Scott Montgomery
Hard Word Book Blog

When Texas Lady Lawyer Merit Bridges does her job for a murdered client a little too well, she finds herself balancing integrity, legal prowess and survival against an adversary whose only goals are vengeance and power. A well-crafted thriller from a writer who truly knows the legal game.

—Judge Debra H. Goldstein,
Sarah Blair Mysteries

Praise for Dollar Signs...

"A high-speed storyline full of twists and turns upon a stark background of reality as lawyers might really experience it. Manning Wolfe is one of the up and coming legal thriller writers of this generation. Read her and enjoy her, but don't expect much sleep!"

— John Ellsworth,
Thaddeus Murfee Legal Thrillers

"Manning Wolfe's new legal thriller is filled with great local color, fascinating characters, legal shenanigans, and plenty of action. A great read, and Texas crime fiction has a new star."

— Bill Crider,
Dan Rhodes Mysteries

"This fast-moving thriller pits Merit Bridges, an engaging and gutsy Texas lawyer, against a bad guy determined to do her in. Readers will revel in this well-plotted page-turner's vivid local Austin setting."

— Helen Currie Foster,
Alice MacDonald Greer Mysteries

"A legal thriller not to be missed, compelling and action-packed, with vivid characters and an authentic Austin setting. Manning Wolfe just put herself on my list of must-read authors."

— Mark Pryor,
Hugo Marston Novels

"Dollar Signs is an "out of the gate" legal thriller that captures everything I like to see from an experienced author. A heroine with a small legal practice takes on a big Texas law firm and gets caught up in arson, murder, and threats to her life. A fast-moving plot and well-developed characters will leave you wanting to read the next thriller in the series. The eyes of Texas will be on Manning Wolfe."

— Rick Polad,
Spencer Manning Mysteries

"This book grabbed me in sentence number one and never let go. The story is about bad people doing dastardly deeds and everyday good people standing up for what's right. It was believable, full of heart, and paced exactly right. Move over, John Grisham. There's a lady lawyer in town."

— Elizabeth Garcia,
Deputy Ricos Tales

"What begins as a not-so-simple arson over a bad sign lease deal quickly spins out of control in Manning Wolfe's Austin-based legal suspense-thriller, Dollar Signs. The pages smoke like burnt fried chicken grease on a Saturday night as the battle royal between Austin lawyer Merit Bridges and her cowboy boot-wearing con man nemesis, Boots King, heats up to the flash point. Austin not only has another world-class author on its hands, we've got a writer who walks the walk and talks the talk, and knows how to mix the ingredients of our Central Texas weird dreams first-hand. This one, my friends, is a non-putter-downer! Mark me down for her next book, 'cause let me tell you, I'm sold."

— George Wier,
Bill Travis Mysteries

"In Dollar Signs, David launches a shot across the bow at Goliath as Manning Wolfe shows that she knows how to zoom the pieces around the chessboard. This novel is smart, funny, moving, and entertaining as hell."

— Jesse Sublett,
1960's Austin Gangsters

"Dollar Signs is a fast-paced thriller pitting Austin attorney Merit Bridges against Boots King, a shadowy henchman. This no-nonsense Texas Lady Lawyer knows her way around a wine list as well as she knows her way around the legal system. Manning Wolfe has assembled an engaging cast of supporting characters, including office manager Betty, who keeps everybody on track amid a cloud of down home wise crackery. Buckle up and enjoy this E-ticket ride all the way to the end!"

— Bill Rodgers,
History Retweets Itself - Humor Series

MUSIC NOTES

Texas Lady Lawyer vs L. A. Baron

a novel by

MANNING WOLFE

STARPATH BOOKS, LLC

Starpath Books, LLC
Austin, TX
www.starpathbooks.com

Library of Congress Cataloging-in Publication Data

Paperback ISBN: 978-1-944225-04-9
Ebook ISBN: 978-1-944225-05-6
LCN: 2017917722

Cover Design by Heidi Dorey
Book Design by Deena Rae - EBookBuilders

Manufactured in the United States of America
10 9 8 7 6 5 4 3 2 1

ACKNOWLEDGEMENTS

Thank you to all who contributed to the content and writing of this book. Much appreciation to those who provided blurbs, musical expertise and encouragement.

Special thanks to Bill Rodgers and Jean Springer.

For Darling Bill, Magical Aaron, and all the other talented Texas musicians.

MUSIC NOTES

Texas Lady Lawyer vs L. A. Baron

MERIT BRIDGES LEGAL THRILLER #2

A lot of country music is sad. I think most art comes out of poverty and hard times. It applies to music. Three chords and the truth – that's what a country song is.

Oh, I think it's definitely Spiritual. All music is. I think it's maybe one of the highest forms of spirituality.

—WILLIE NELSON

1

On a beautiful Texas spring day, Merit Bridges found herself in a situation she never thought she'd be - a fist fight. She wrestled against her attacker's six-foot frame and found herself overwhelmed by his strength. He grabbed her from behind with an arm around her shoulders. Merit spun free, ducked to avoid a punch to the face, and popped back up with a jab to his chin. He shook his head and steadied himself. Merit took advantage of his disorientation, grabbed him from behind in a bear hug with her legs around his waist and held his arms in place. He spun around and around until she lost her grip, detached and dropped to the ground. She hopped to her feet and swung. He blocked her jab, and punched her in the stomach. Merit lost her breath and doubled over. Her attacker laughed at the amazed look on her face.

"You hit me!" Merit said.

"You hit me," Mayor Taylor said.

Both held their red boxing gloves in the air proclaiming double victory and laughed out at the crowd of over fifty thousand. A banner above them displayed in huge red letters: TEXAS KNOCKOUT ILLITERACY!

"We're calling it a draw." Mayor Taylor said into the microphone. "Let me thank Merit Bridges, Austin attorney, fundraiser extraordinaire, and one of our favorite University of Texas Longhorns."

The crowd clapped as Merit made the Hook 'em Horns sign and joined Mayor Taylor at the microphone to address the audience. The sea of milling partiers spread from Barton Springs Road to Lady Bird Lake and covered almost every square foot of grass across the expanse known as Auditorium Shores in Austin, Texas. Attendees milled about between stages, lay on blankets in the grass, and perched in folding canvas chairs. They drank beer in recycled plastic cups and ate various types of food from barbecue sandwiches to food truck tacos to corn on the cob dripping with butter sauce.

Mayor Taylor and Merit bumped gloved fists, then she turned and spoke into the microphone.

"Thank you all for being here today and for supporting our three charities in the fifth annual music festival. Thanks to our sponsors, each of our musical performers, and the runners who participated in the 10K this morning. Last, but not least, thanks to Mayor Taylor for being our master of ceremonies and a really good sport."

The audience applauded and laughed. Television cameras zoomed in and drones snapped shots of the crowd from above. A small plane flew overhead trailing a banner proclaiming: TEXAS READS!

A second banner hung on the temporary fencing near the stage: Austin Charity Music Festival benefiting: Reading for the Blind & Dyslexic, Fresh Start for Kindergarten Readers, and Reading for the Incarcerated.

"Thank you Merit for chairing the event again this year. At last count, we've raised over one million dollars to be distributed among the three charities."

Merit stepped off the stage in her hot pink silk boxing shorts and white knee high socks. Her blonde ponytail swung from side to side as she climbed down the steps. Mayor Taylor, in black silks and 'The Old Pecan Street Cafe' t-shirt, continued to work the audience, also known as future voters. Merit kept an eye on the mayor as she entered the VIP tent to check on the next act, a five-piece rockabilly band out of East Austin called Killer Delight. She nodded at Valentine Berry Louis, her law clerk, who was also a volunteer, as he gathered the rock group in a corner and went over instructions from a clipboard.

Bo, the lead singer, looked at Merit from bottom to top. He stopped at her eyes and they held there for a brief moment until a gel neck-wrap noodle interrupted his gaze when it passed before Merit's face and broke the spell.

Ace, Merit's teenage son and only child, smiled his million-dollar smile and handed out gel neck-wraps and bottles of water from a silver Yeti cooler. Ace wore the official t-shirt for the event which showed the black bats flying out from under the Congress Avenue Bridge and turning into music notes.

"Saw the mayor kick your ass, Mom," Ace said.

"Yeah, watch your language, Peaches. Give me one of those. I'm about to boil in this heat," Merit said.

Ace playfully hit his mother on the shoulder with the wet cooling tube and laughed. She'd been a single mom for some time now and the closeness of their relationship showed in their playfulness.

Merit wrapped the gel noodle around her neck and downed half a bottle of water until it flowed over her chin and down the front of her shirt.

"Easy, Mom, you'll get sick," Ace said.

"Who's the parent here?" Merit laughed.

Ace was in town for the event from his school in Houston for dyslexic students. It was good to have him home and Merit beamed at him like the proud parent she was. Joy and Tucker, Merit's best friends in Houston, had driven Ace up for the event. It was great having a houseful of fun loving guests.

Merit had been working on the festival committee for several years and had been an advocate for literacy since she'd discovered Ace's learning disability when he was in fifth grade.

A thin young man with purple hair walked toward Merit and Ace. Purple Hair looked like every other band member in the VIP tent - baggy jeans, t-shirt, no belt. Merit's armpits prickled ever so slightly. This visceral indicator of danger or intuition alert had been with her since she was a child. At this moment, she wasn't sure if something was up or if the Texas heat was giving her a heat rash. As Purple Hair got closer she saw that his clothes were dirty and his hair needed washing.

Ag, a tall, cool drink of water, with the kind of eyelashes women spent time and money to buy, stepped between Purple Hair and Merit.

"Where's your badge?" Ag Malone asked.

"I'm with the band," Purple Hair said.

"I don't think so," Ag said.

"I just want to talk to Ms. Bridges," Purple Hair said.

"You can't be in here without a VIP badge. Security reasons. You'll have to leave." Ag said as he escorted the interloper by his elbow to the nearest exit.

Merit was glad that Albert "Ag" Malone was doing his job. Ag was her private investigator for the Law Office of Merit Bridges, and coordinating security for the VIP portion of the festival. He wore his standard maroon shirt and jeans, a uniform of sorts for him, which showed his allegiance to Texas A&M University, his alma mater. Ag was long and lean with a quiet demeanor that was mysterious and attractive.

After Ag had ejected Purple Hair, Merit signaled to Val.

"The mayor is wrapping it up. Let's get Killer Delight up on stage as soon as he's finished," Merit said.

"All set," Val said and moved the band over by the stage entry ramp. He appeared almost too thin as he adjusted his vintage Tom Selleck type shorts and cropped Liberty Lunch retro t-shirt.

The crowd caught a peek through the tent opening at Bo Harding, the lead singer, and let out a roar.

On stage, Mayor Taylor got the hint as Merit moved back up the ramp toward him. Killer Delight held at the bottom of the stairs and the crowd roared again.

"Thank you all once more for your support this year for our very worthy charities. I'll now turn the mic over to Merit Bridges," Mayor Taylor said.

Merit stepped up to the microphone and raised her hand.

"Thank you all again for being here," Merit said. "We'll end the event with a killer local band that really needs no introduction.

Without further ado, here is the band you've all been waiting for, Killer Delight!"

The audience surged toward the barriers in front of the bandstand and attendees moved away from the other four stages around the lake and toward the main stage to see the lead act of the event and the hottest band in Austin.

Purple Hair tried to go against the crowd, was pushed about and fell. Several attendees helped him up and he worked his way toward the main exit on Barton Springs Road.

Red Thallon stood in the center of the festival crowd with microphone in hand. Her gimme cap had the Austin9Online logo on it. She continued her interview with a young woman with a large tattooed curl of barbed wire climbing out of her blouse and wrapping around her neck.

"Are you enjoying the festival?" Red asked.

"Loving it," said the young woman.

"How many acts have you been able to watch?" Red asked.

"I've seen six so far today including Solange, Erica Badu, and the Derailers. I'm looking forward to Killer Delight," the young woman said and pointed to the main stage.

The crowd roared as Killer Delight tuned up with a familiar chord and Red had to yell into the microphone to be heard.

"Thanks for stopping to chat," Red said and turned full face to the camera. "Catch us tonight on Austin9Online and at ten on KNEW nightly news. We'll have live interviews with Bob Schneider and Kevin Price. For now, let's have a listen to Killer Delight."

The camera panned the cheering crowd and moved toward the stage settling on a close-up of Bo Harding. The tall muscular rock star was wearing denim shirt and pants plus a pair of red leather and rhinestone cowboy boots. He shook back his long dark blonde hair and struck a strong riff on his guitar. The audience went wild again, and the concert began.

After Killer Delight had finished their set and the crowds had dispersed, Merit and Val sorted out the aftermath in the VIP tent and looked around for any remaining volunteers to help.

Liam Nolan, an aging, long-haired, tanned faced guitarist with a purple guitar pick in the band of his tan straw cowboy hat stood outside the flap of the VIP tent. He put out a cigarette and chugged down a bottle of water. He looked like a worn-out rock star that some people thought they recognized but weren't sure from where. The seasoned music lovers knew him, of course. He was trying to redeem himself for years of alcoholism and drug abuse by giving back at the festival. His Narcotics Anonymous sponsor constantly reminded him that the twelve steps ended with service.

"Liam, if you're up for it, let's open all the flaps and let in the roadies." Val said.

"Glad to help," Liam said.

Merit saw Bo Harding and other members of Killer Delight walk over and shake Liam's hand.

"I grew up on your music, man," Bo said. "It got me through some rough times."

"Hey, thanks," Liam said and bumped fists with Bo.

"I saw your act at Stubb's once. Great show," Bo said.

"Those were good times," Liam said.

"If you ever decide to start writing songs again, keep me in mind. I love a good lyric," Bo said.

Merit had been helping Liam sort out his business affairs and put his financial life in order again. It was a slow process. Val was assisting by chronicling Liam's portfolio of songs from years of writing. Some had sold and some were still in old dust covered suitcases and boxes in her conference room.

"Just a minute Bo. Val, do I have anything left to sell?" Liam grinned.

Merit smiled and kept sorting through leftover t-shirts with Ace.

Val laughed. Merit knew he would never answer such a question even in jest if he wanted to continue to work in the law office. Confidentiality was her first rule for her staff. Integrity was her first rule for herself.

Merit recalled that while cataloguing and organizing Liam's songs, she and Val had discovered and hummed new tunes on the list that they recognized. They were surprised again and again that Liam had authored the songs that were part of the emerging portfolio.

Liam was the real deal. How he wound up barely surviving and in NA meetings every day was a story he didn't share with many except Merit. He had finally gotten control of his life. Liam's future was in his hands, or so he thought.

2

Liam sat at the edge of Lady Bird Lake near the statue of Stevie Ray Vaughan at four-thirty in the morning. The crowds had long cleared from the festival and the city was settled for the night. The ember from his cigarette glowed in the pre-dawn light. He looked at the skyline of Austin reflected in the dark water with his Fender Stratocaster nestled in its case at his feet.

After the festival, he'd sat in on a set with some old classic Austin musicians at the Saxon Pub before finding his way back to the lake. He ran his hands over the guitar case and thought of the horn shape that gave the axe its balance and distinctive look. It was his favorite possession and one of the few he had not pawned or sold to cover his former habit. His addiction to various drugs culminating in Fentanyl had cost him everything except his life and one remaining Strat. Fortunately, he got into recovery before he could sell his entire portfolio of music. There were huge gaps in his memory and millions of dollars lost who knew where. With no family and a loveless bed, he was lonely but increasingly hopeful. His NA sponsor and a few remaining friends, including Merit, were a big support for him and taking life one day at a time helped him to manage his life in small bites.

Liam watched two teenagers with handheld controllers work their way down to the water's edge flying their drones over the lake and then under the bridges that crossed over the water at regular intervals.

Liam twirled a purple guitar pick between his fingers. It had a series of quarter notes on one side and L.N. on the other side. He thought of it as his business card. It was his signature gift to fans, and his talisman when he wanted a cool way to introduce himself.

He heard bits of conversation as the skinny male teens passed a joint back and forth. They laughed and played with their flying toys that looked like four legged spiders.

"Great light," said the first teen with ginger colored hair.

"Magic hour," said the other teen, sporting a mouth full of metal braces.

"Here come the cops."

"Throw the roach in the water."

Two extremely fit policemen on bicycles rode along the shoreline and spun gravel when they stopped beside the teens. Their uniforms were navy blue with shorts in lieu of long pants and they both had Blueguns tasers on their duty belts instead of a gun. Their bicycles were fitted with saddlebags holding first aid equipment.

"What are you two doing out here at this hour?" the older policeman said.

"We're capturing the light, officer," ginger teen said.

"Right," said the younger policeman sniffing the air.

"You have a license for that drone?" the older policeman said.

"No sir. I'm just taking pics for fun. No commercial use," ginger teen said.

"We don't need a license," braces teen said and giggled.

The two policemen looked at each other and appeared to make a non-verbal decision.

"Wrap it up and get on out of here." The younger policeman said.

"Yes, sir," ginger teen said.

The policemen rode on through the area, nodded at Liam, crossed over the bridge and then patrolled the other side of the lake. There was little activity, but the water's edge was never totally quiet in Austin.

Liam played the lyrics of a new song over and over in his mind. He smelled the wet earth at the edge of the water, listed the Twelve Steps in his mind, and lingered on gratitude. He felt light and unburdened now that he was finally turning his life around. He was grateful to be alive. Maybe he would write a song for Killer Delight, earn some money, and make a comeback. Possibly perform at Antone's or Guero's again. Maybe he'd meet a nice woman. Why not? Everything was possible again.

Liam got up, picked up his Strat, and walked along the lake on the hike and bike trail toward home. As he dropped down under the First Street Bridge, he looked up from his dreamy state to see a Pursuer coming toward him. The Pursuer was slight in stature, but backlit by the bridge and Liam could only see an outline.

"Hey, Liam," the Pursuer said.

"Hey. Who's there?" Liam asked.

"Don't you know who I am?" the Pursuer asked.

The voice sounded familiar. The Pursuer continued toward Liam until they were close enough for Liam to recognize the face.

"What are you doing here at this hour?" Liam asked.

"Looking for you. I followed you from the Saxon Pub."

"Well you found me. What do you want? I told you I have nothing for you," Liam said.

"Don't be that way. Let me buy you a cup of coffee. I want to talk to you," the Pursuer said.

"I don't want coffee and I don't want to talk to you. Leave me alone," Liam said and turned to go.

"Don't turn your back on me again!"

The Pursuer looked around and picked up a large rock from beside the path. Liam felt movement behind him. As he turned back, he felt a strong blow between his neck and skull. He fell, dropped his guitar case, then struggled to get up.

"You, asshole," Liam said.

As Liam pushed himself up from the ground, the Pursuer grabbed the guitar case and slammed it into Liam's head. Liam fell to the ground again and the Pursuer hit him with the case over and over until the latches broke and the case flew open, sending the Strat spiraling into the water.

Liam looked up to see the Pursuer freeze, blink, and begin to shake. A hand reached down by the dying face and gathered up the case handle and rock, and put them inside the broken case. The Pursuer ran along the trees and out of the park with the case. Liam's blood spread out over the trail, pooled at the grassy edge, and finally spilled over into the dark water.

No one came to help poor Liam or see the face of his killer. Dozens of purple guitar picks lay strewn along the water's edge.

The next morning, Red Thallon stood at the site of the murder of Liam Nolan. The serene water of Lady Bird Lake lapped quietly against the bank. Downtown Austin glistened in the background in the morning sun.

She raised the microphone to her mouth as the cameraman counted down five, four, three, then went quiet and held up two fingers, then one finger pointed at Red.

"We are at the site of the murder of Liam Nolan, an Austin favorite for his rock and roll hits of the Eighties and Nineties. Nolan was apparently assaulted in attempt to obtain his expensive Stratocaster guitar. The mugger was unsuccessful, as the instrument was found in the water after the incident," Red said.

Several lookers gathered around the yellow and black tape marking off the crime scene as the camera went to wide angle and showed the area. The cameraman scanned the audience and paused on each face. The young man with purple hair stared with wide eyes at the scene.

"Austin police are asking anyone with information to come forward. More on Austin9Online and at five on KNEW" Red said.

She made a slicing motion across her throat.

"That's a wrap."

3

Ornette Coleman Baron, known in the music business as L.A. Baron, stepped out of his big black Cadillac Escalade dressed from head to toe in designer black topped by a black leather bomber jacket. He was followed by three minions fawning to do his bidding. All three wore the same uniform of black pants, black t-shirts and heavy chains around their necks with some type of medallion on the end. L.A. stayed apart from his entourage. He didn't like walking next to someone he had to look up to see. The only thing L.A. couldn't buy was more height. Napoleonic by nature, he made up for his diminutive stature by wielding power.

Ornette had been nicknamed L.A. by his clients when he first moved to Los Angeles to work in the music and video gaming business. He liked the name immediately and perpetuated the moniker until everyone in the biz thought of it as his real initials. Although he had attended Washington University Law School, his family in St. Louis had unwittingly geared him for the music world by naming him after his mother's favorite saxophonist.

If one was in the music biz, one knew of L.A. and vied for an opportunity to meet him. He wasn't the most nurturing manager by reputation. In fact, he was considered tough to work with, but he had a great ear. He was as successful as any manager who'd come before him, and his goal was to surpass every icon in the music world. There was no doubt in L.A.'s mind that he could accomplish that goal. He would do whatever it took. Anything.

His role model, unbeknownst to anyone but himself, was Colonel Tom Parker who had managed Elvis Presley since the early days of rock and roll in the 1950s. Parker was L.A.'s template for the all-controlling-mastermind style that he used today. The dysfunctional marriage of Parker and Elvis was not something to be avoided but was desired by L.A. He was sure that Elvis would never have made it to the top without Parker. Just as he was sure that his bands would not make it without him. Some of them agreed.

L.A. and his entourage entered a high-rise glass and metal building that looked like a giant phallus with a treble clef on the side. The reception signage read: Baron Entertainment Enterprises, and the building directory showed L.A. to be officed in the penthouse at the top of forty-three floors.

"Hey, L.A.," Minion One said, looking at his phone, "Says on Facebook that old geezer Liam you represent was murdered in Austin."

L.A. stopped, then recovered and continued.

"Is that so?" L.A. said. "Overdose?"

"No. Looks like he was bludgeoned to death while he was walking home."

"When?" Minion Two asked.

"Last night or rather early this morning. Some Texas lady lawyer named Merit Bridges gave a statement that he was clean and sober. Twelve Steps. Getting his act together and all that."

The group entered the elevator setting their bling to jingling. Minion Two pushed *P* for penthouse, as the doors closed.

"Hmmm," L.A. said and sent a reproachful look to Ash Joyner, his number one and the first minion in the pack.

"Says it's probably a mugging. Beat the shit of him."

"Maybe he deserved it," L.A. said.

When the doors opened on the top floor, L.A. entered his office and the minions scurried like rats to their respective cubicles to wait by the intercom for L.A.'s next command.

As they left the office, Minion Two whispered to Minion Three, "Baron does mean powerful overlord."

Minion Three smirked. "Yeah, and he also has the money."

"Payday is only a week away," Minion Two said.

"Resume' will be built in a year," Minion One said.

L.A. pretended not to hear them.

"Close the door behind you," he said.

L.A. went further into his inner sanctum. It was a large room filled with chrome, glass, and leather. In the far corner was a small black door marked *PRIVATE* with a metal keypad by the door handle.

L.A. opened his computer contact list and speed dialed a number in the 512 area code.

"Law Office of Merit Bridges," the voice said on the other end of the line.

"L.A. Baron calling for Merit Bridges," L.A. said into the speaker.

After a pause, he heard Merit come on the line.

"How may I help you, Mr. Baron?" Merit said.

"Hello, Ms. Bridges. I'm a music manager in Los Angeles. I'm calling about the funeral for Liam Nolan," L.A. said.

"I've seen your name in Liam's documents. There's no one to consult about the arrangements yet. I mean no one has come forward. He didn't have a family. His wishes were to be cremated and ashes spread along Lady Bird Lake, but the body is still with the coroner," Merit said.

"What happened?" L.A. asked.

"The police are still not sure. May have been an attempt to steal his guitar that went sideways. But that's just a guess," Merit said.

"Will the funeral be in Austin? I have an office there and can leave any time," L.A. said.

"I don't know when we'll have detailed arrangements, but I'll be sure to have someone call you when it's set up. I'm sorry for your loss."

"Loss? Yeah, thanks. What about his estate?" L.A. asked.

"That's what I mean by no one to ask. We had just begun to put together an inventory of his assets," Merit said. "He hadn't executed a will yet."

"Well, I have a will from when I worked with him and I guess that's the one that we'll probate," L.A. said.

Merit's armpits prickled.

"Afraid to disappoint," Merit said. She started to get the feeling that L.A. was not as nice as he tried to seem. "Liam revoked all prior wills and codicils in writing when we started the process of sorting his assets. I'm afraid he died intestate."

"That's convenient," L.A. said confirming her assessment of his tone.

"Not really. I know his wishes, but he hadn't signed the new last will and testament yet," Merit said.

"What about his wife?" L.A. said.

"He wasn't married. I assumed you knew," Merit said. "I'm afraid that's all I can tell you at this point. Everything else is confidential until a judge releases the information through probate."

"When will that be?" L.A. said.

"I guess we'd better handle the funeral first. I'll have someone get in touch with the details," Merit said and hung up.

No wonder Liam was getting rid of you, Merit thought.

4

Police surrounded and protected a small crowd at the edge of Auditorium Shores near the memorial to Stevie Ray Vaughan, with downtown Austin as the backdrop for the sad event. Stevie Ray's face was shaded by his signature hat, and the rock and roll icon's permanent metal shadow reflected the sunlight. Someone had added fresh purple tulips to Stevie Ray's outstretched hand, which held the neck of his metal guitar.

A dark pottery urn sat at the edge of the limestone base of the statue surrounded by bouquets of flowers. Each musician in the group approached the urn quietly and placed a guitar pick at the edge of the vessel.

Merit stood quietly with Ag, Val, and Betty from her office. Merit wore a light tan linen dress and Val had on an Oscar de la Renta vintage suit in a blue and white striped seersucker fabric. Betty wore her best summer St. John's knit suit and extra Aqua Net on her beehive hairdo. Ag had on his usual jeans and Aggie maroon starched shirt.

All four were somber and mournful as they'd grown fond of Liam and known him in a way few had - sober. To Merit and her staff Liam had been a kind man who just wanted peace in the later part of his life. Maybe a little more music and someone to love. Not much, a simple existence with no accolades or dramas to set him off on his roller coaster of drug use again. Their four hearts beat a song of unified bereavement that each understood in the other.

To most of the gathering and the public at large, Liam was known as a partier and wild man who had rocked the music world a few decades earlier with his music. He was especially known for his hit song, *Fever Stomp*. It was rarely played anymore, and basically undiscovered by the current generation of hip-hop artists and new style rockers. Occasionally Merit would hear a modified version overhead in an elevator or on a retro jukebox like the one at Shady Grove Cafe.

L.A. Baron, in all black, stood in front of three other men in similar dress. The minions were careful not to crowd L.A. and never touched him. L.A. was across the venue from Merit with his arms folded across his chest and his big black sunglasses covering his eyes and most of his face. The black garb and shiny medallions drew the Texas sun and he and the minions began to sweat almost immediately.

The remaining crowd was comprised of old hippies who had helped keep Austin weird, a few hipsters who had heard Liam's music in Austin bars, and a few very famous musicians from the old guard of rock and roll.

Merit saw what appeared to be a woman passenger sitting in a dark blue car parked in the nearest lot with the window rolled down a couple of inches. Cigarette smoke curled out of the small opening in the glass. A burly man was behind the wheel.

Purple Hair peeked at the group from behind the trunk of a nearby tree. He was surrounded by several curious souls who had happened upon the open-air funeral while taking their daily walk. Several dogs looked on, well behaved on their leashes.

They possibly sense the somberness of the occasion, Merit thought.

Merit stood before the group and shared her comments with the crowd. "Thank you for coming today. It's hard to believe that we were just near here a few days ago for such a joyful event. Liam contributed to the festival as his way of giving back to a community that had been so good to him. He would have been happy to see you all here. Although Liam was a recent acquaintance and client, he was endearing and special and quickly becoming a friend. I wish him Godspeed. Now, let me ask Liam's NA sponsor, Reverend Morton Hightower to say a few words."

A tall lanky man in a suit with a long coat that looked like it came from the Salvation Army stepped in front of the group.

"I knew Liam for a very short time, since his recent return to Austin. He was a good man and was growing every day in his inner work and spiritual development. We can all be comforted by the fact that he'd found peace. His music will live on in our lives and hearts as a gentle reminder of him and his talent."

Hightower said a few more comforting words to the crowd. Merit stepped forward, thanked him and introduced Bo Harding. Bo wore a pair of jeans, cowboy boots, and a vintage Stephen Bruton t-shirt. His dark blonde hair was pulled back in a black leather tie.

Bo steadied himself, hummed a note, then delivered an a cappella version of Willie Nelson's *Blue Eyes Cryin' In the Rain* that set the group to fumbling for tissues in pockets and purses.

After the song ended and a moment of silence passed, Merit stepped to the water's edge behind the monumental Stevie Ray, opened and upended the urn containing Liam's ashes, and set his remains free to merge with his own blood in the flowing blue water glistening at the edge of downtown Austin in the morning sun.

5

A week later, Merit parked her new charcoal gray BMW SUV on the street in front of Austin High School. She'd recently made the purchase after a low down dirty dog named Boots King had wiped out her white BMW while attempting to take her life on the beach in Port Aransas.

Merit took a small folding stool, her camera bag, and her briefcase out of the hatch. She had on a pair of jogging shorts, a sports bra and a tie-dyed Chuy's Tex-Mex t-shirt featuring a gecko and the ever-popular slogan: *Keep Austin Weird*. Merit still managed to keep one foot in old hippie Austin and one foot in new hip Austin although it was becoming more and more difficult as the influx of new residents continued to swarm the city. She crossed over to the hike and bike trail along the north shore of the Colorado River where it met Lady Bird Lake. It was a perfect day. The water was full of paddle boarders, kayakers, canoers and scullers. She walked along the trail and located a deteriorating wooden picnic table with two women sitting behind it.

"Morning, ladies. Beautiful day. Do we have any clients?" Merit asked.

Both women smiled. Elizabeth was a family law practitioner and Julie was board certified in real estate. Both were dressed in running clothes similar to Merit's with their hair pulled back and

21

no makeup on their faces. Julie was sweaty and unkempt as if she'd already been for a jog.

"A few customers have come by," Elizabeth said.

"Yep," Julie said and stood up.

Merit set her briefcase and other bags on the table.

"If you two have it, my shift is over," Julie said.

"Good to go," Merit said.

"See you next month," Julie said and gathered her belongings and backpack.

Merit had been volunteering with Austin Legal Advantage, a non-profit serving the indigent, for over a year. Part of her responsibilities included giving free advice once a month on Saturday mornings on the hike and bike trail and one evening a month at the Austin Legal Clinic on Martin Luther King Boulevard. The idea had come from a local attorney who represented the homeless, but found that most of them would not come into the office because of their appearance and fear of being removed by security. The open air also helped a little with the sweaty clothes and odors due to poor hygiene and living conditions. Merit much preferred the open-air hike and bike trail duty to the close quarters of the nighttime duty downtown.

A woman with a baby on her hip and two small children at her legs approached the table.

"I've got this one," Elizabeth said. "Probably a family law matter."

Merit set out her clipboard with sign-up sheet and a stack of brochures from Austin Legal Advantage. Seeing no one to advise, she began working through her email and social media sites on her big ass iPhone. She still hadn't gotten used to carrying it around since the plus sized phones had come out. She didn't have long to wait before her first customer arrived.

A very dirty man with a natty beard and dreadlocks approached the table with a stack of folded papers in his soiled hands. He kept his bearded face down and did not make eye contact with Merit.

"May I help you?" Merit asked.

"I have a question about a deed," the unkempt man said and put the papers on the table.

"Be glad to take a look," Merit said. "Please sign in on the clip board."

The man made an X on the designated line.

"That'll do," Merit said, opened his documents and read the first page.

"My friend Slag said I could come by and see you," he said.

"Slag's a good man. He's been a client of mine for a long time." Merit said.

"Slag said that. I got this from my mother before she died," the man said and gestured toward the paperwork.

"Was her name Emily Jo Johnson?"

"Yes, see right there," he pointed at the top of the page.

"And are you Gilbert Mansard Johnson?"

"Yep, that's me. Call me Gilbert."

"It says here that your mother deeded a house in East Austin to you in 1964. Did you ever take possession of the house?" Merit asked.

"I live there now, but it's condemned and an architect wants to buy it," Gilbert said.

"Have you kept up the taxes? Are there any liens?" Merit asked.

"I owe back taxes, that's how the architect found me. He said he was researching the records because the city is about to foreclose on the house."

"I see. It may be a good time to sell then," Merit said.

"I want to make sure it's all legal," Gilbert said.

"I can help you with this. Let me scan a few of these pages with my phone and I'll ask a title company to run the lot and block numbers and see where you stand."

Merit opened the TurboScan app on her phone and centered the screen over each page and clicked. She checked to make sure she could read the scanned copies of the documents, then handed them back to Gilbert.

"I should have the results in a few days. Give me a call and I'll let you know what you can legally do. Here's my card," Merit said.

"Thank you," Gilbert said and took the card. "I can pay you if I sell the house."

"No need. This is all free. If it goes beyond a simple property check, we'll work out some type of payment plan," Merit said.

"I'd like the architect to call you. Can you tell him what's legal and that you'll be lookin' out for me?" Gilbert asked.

"I'll be glad to. Just give him the same number that's on the card and tell him I'm reviewing your documents and researching your title," Merit said.

Gilbert smiled for the first time and revealed gaps in lieu of his top four middle teeth. He walked off whistling softly with the documents extended before him as if on a tray.

♪

No one new came along, so Merit took advantage of the break, crossed the street near her car to the bathrooms then returned to the table. She caught sight of a thin young man standing by the edge of the woods at the water's edge. He seemed to be watching her.

"My shift's up, I'm heading out for a run," Elizabeth said.

"Enjoy. I'll hold the fort for another hour and see if anyone else shows up," Merit said.

Merit continued with her email and phone work as several running teams dripping in sweat turned the corner and crossed the bridge over the lake. She emailed Gilbert's scanned documents to Betty with a note to start the title search.

She didn't have long to wait until her next customer arrived.

The thin young man that Merit thought she recognized approached the hike and bike trail from the trees along the shoreline. He was dirty and sweaty and had shades of faded purple color in his tangled hair that was mostly in dreadlocks. Merit couldn't place him. He looked around the parking area and trail, hesitated, then approached Merit at the advice table. As he came closer, Merit recognized him as the purple haired attendee from the charity music festival that Ag had removed during the Killer Delight concert.

"Is that woman gone? Are you leaving too? Purple Hair asked.

Merit's armpits prickled with unmistakable information from her intuition to pay attention.

"Not yet. May I help you?" Merit asked.

She studied his face and was surprised at how young he looked.

"I've been trying to find you. I called your office," Purple Hair said.

"I get a lot of calls. Did you leave a message?"

"Nope."

"I think I remember you from the concert. Were you in the VIP tent?"

"Yeah. I tried to ask you a question, but that security guy threw me out."

"Ag. That's his job."

"I guess."

"Well, you're here now. You went to a lot of effort to talk to me. What can I do for you? Do you have a legal question?" Merit asked.

"I do. It's about Liam Nolan. You're his lawyer, aren't you?"

"Yes. I was. Now I work for the estate. We just had his funeral last week," Merit said.

"Yeah. I was there. You said nice things about him."

"He would have liked that you were there. Are you a musician too?" Merit asked

"Play a little guitar. Mostly acoustic."

Merit nodded. "Do you live down here? Are you homeless?" Merit asked.

"Sometimes. Mostly I stay with other students where I can sneak in after hours. Do I have to be homeless to get advice?"

"No. It's just that you're very young to be living on the streets. What happened?"

"I was a student at the University of Texas. I was suspended for skipping classes and smoking weed. Lost my scholarship."

"UT is a good school. You must be smart."

"Not smart enough, I guess. Got kicked out, didn't I?"

Merit smiled and extended her hand. "I'm Merit Bridges. I am a business attorney. I occasionally am forced into court, but rarely. Hopefully you won't need a litigator. What can I do for you?"

He shook her hand and shifted his weight from one foot to the other.

25

Merit pointed to the line under Gilbert's X on the sheet on the clipboard. "Let's start with your name. Please put it here and sign your name here."

"Why?"

"It's proof that you read the top of the page. See here, it says that I am giving you advice, but on a limited basis because I may not know your entire situation. It also says that I'm not your lawyer even if I help you today."

Davey Ray Bell printed his name in block letters then signed on the next line.

"So, I don't have to pay anything?"

"Not a red cent. I'm giving free advice for another hour, so take your time. What's the problem?"

"I think Liam Nolan may be my father. Was my father," Davey said.

Merit sucked in a breath through parted lips.

Here comes trouble, she thought.

"Can you help me?" Davey asked.

"As far as I know, Liam didn't have any children. What makes you think that you're his son?" Merit asked.

"I have some old papers and photos from my mother, and I've been doing some research. Bell is my mother's maiden name, and I don't think there's a father on my birth certificate."

"Do you have the papers with you?"

"No, I just want to ask today what would happen if he is my father?"

"Do you mean with his estate?"

"No. Yes. I want to know if I can use his name if he's really my father."

"Well, Davey, you can use any name you want if you legally change it in court, but I think you mean you want to claim your heritage."

"Right, I want to prove where I came from."

"I see. You do know that I'm in the process of sorting out his estate?"

"Yeah. I was hoping he said in his will that I was his son."

"We were working on his will when he was murdered."

Davey flinched.

"Sorry, I mean when he died. I think he would have told me if he had fathered a son, but that doesn't mean he didn't have one and was unaware of the fact. You must realize from the funeral comments and obituary that he had a pretty wild life."

"Yeah, I know. I still want to find out."

"Did you see him in the VIP tent?" Merit asked.

"Was he there?" Davey asked.

"Yes. What does your mother say about him?"

"She says… She's just… She's not around much."

The mounted police patrol rode by on their horses and Merit looked up to greet them. When she looked back down, Davey Ray Bell was gone and her stack of business cards were knocked over. A small purple guitar pick was on the table before her.

The next day, Merit exited the elevator and entered The Law Office of Merit Bridges in a high-rise bank building in downtown Austin. She smelled something buttery and delicious.

Betty came around the corner from the break room at the end of a long corridor of individual offices. Each office had the name of an employee on the door or the designation of its use as a closet, conference room or copy room.

"Morning Betty. How are you?" Merit asked.

"Woke up on the right side of the dirt," Betty said.

"Good thing. Are you making breakfast tacos? Glad I ran an extra mile yesterday," Merit said.

Betty handed Merit a cup of tea and took her briefcase.

"Morning' Darlin'. I'll feed you in a minute. Let me walk you to your office," Betty said.

Merit was puzzled.

"Are you handling me again? What's up?" Merit laughed.

"There's a kid named Davey in the break room who needs a bath. Bless his heart, he's on his fourth breakfast taco and I've sent Val to the market for supplies. At this rate, he may go through a dozen eggs."

27

"Oh my," Merit said.

"He says you're his lawyer," Betty said.

"Oh my," Merit said again.

"Have you ever met him?" Betty asked.

"He came to the pro bono table on the hike and bike trail this weekend. He thinks he's Liam Nolan's son," Merit said.

"Oh my," Betty said.

♪

Betty escorted Davey into Merit's office. He wiped his mouth with a napkin and looked for a place to toss it.

"I'll take it, Honey. You sit right here in the guest chair," Betty said and pointed to one of the two leather club chairs in front of Merit's desk.

Betty gave Merit a 'be nice' look as she exited behind Davey and closed the office door.

"So, you found me," Merit said.

"Wasn't hard. I am a UT student. Was. I know how to use a computer and your law firm name was on the card."

"That's right. So what's the plan? You didn't make an appointment. I assume a smart guy like yourself would know to do that."

"You might not have agreed to see me. Besides, my phone's cut off. Couldn't pay the bill," Davey said.

"Hmm," Merit said. She thought of making a remark involving a pay phone but thought better of arguing about where he might find one in Austin.

"Are you safe? Do you have a place to live yet?"

"Sure. I'm covered with my buddy Kevin," Davey said.

Merit looked at him with a question mark in her eyes. "Well?" Merit said.

"So, what do we do now?" Davey asked.

"That depends on you. Are you asserting a claim against Liam Nolan's estate?"

"Yes, yes, I am. How do I do that?" Davey asked.

"Did you bring any proof of your claim?" Merit asked.

"Not with me, but I have it stashed away," Davey said.

"We proceed depending on your documentation. It may take DNA testing to prove paternity," Merit said.

"How does that work?" Davey asked.

"A lab is given a swab or blood sample to test in order to determine the biological father of a child. We will need a chain of custody DNA paternity test if we ultimately plan to use it in court," Merit said. "Not just informational which just gives us the yes or no."

"How accurate is it?" Davey asked.

"About ninety-nine percent," Merit said.

"What do I do?" Davey asked.

"Pretty simple. I'd have you set up an appointment with Ag, my investigator that you met at the concert. He can escort you to a lab he trusts for accuracy. They'll rub the inside of your cheeks to obtain epithelial cells. Then they compare them to Liam's DNA," Merit said.

"What does it cost?" Davey asked.

"A couple of hundred bucks," Merit said.

"How long does it take?" Davey asked.

"About three to five days after they get both samples," Merit said.

"I can't pay for it. Maybe there's a free clinic somewhere," Davey said.

"It's very inexpensive. I don't think the probate court would have an objection to the expenditure if you can't pay for it," Merit said.

"Let's do it," Davey said.

"You probably need a lawyer, and since I'm handling the Liam Nolan estate, I can't represent you without leave of court."

"I don't want another lawyer. You're the only lawyer I know. How do we leave the court?" Davey asked.

"It's leave of court. It's a legal term. It means the court could give you special permission to hire me and they will give me protection from the estate due to a possible conflict between you and any possible members of the estate. It probably won't happen, but I know plenty of lawyers I can refer you to. Most likely the judge will let me work in concert with your attorney."

"I'd like you to work in concert. Who would be a member of the estate?" Dave asked.

"Parents, spouses, brothers and sisters, cousins. Any relative really. Liam indicated that he didn't have any living relatives."

"There weren't any," Davey said.

"How do you know? You're claiming to be his child, maybe there are others with claims."

"He didn't have any. I checked while I was following him around," Davey said.

"You were following him?" Merit was alarmed.

"Yeah. I tried to talk to him."

"When? Where?" Merit asked.

"Around," Davey said.

"Do the police know this?" Merit asked.

"I don't know. Why? Should they?" Davey asked.

"I hope not," Merit said.

6

Ag drove from downtown to Airport Boulevard and Highway 183. Traffic was heavy as usual. He pulled into the Texas Office of Vital Records on Levander Loop, parked, went in, and got in line.

"I need to request a birth certificate and a death certificate. I need the full-sized long form," Ag said.

"Fill out each of these forms and I need photo identification," the clerk said.

"I pre-printed the forms and filled them out, and here's my I.D.," Ag said.

"Take a seat, it'll be a few minutes," the clerk said.

Ag sat in a row of molded plastic chairs and looked around. The clerk was one of those gray-haired government employees who'd been with the state for thirty years and was likely waiting for retirement.

Probably has five or six pictures of grandkids and cats on her desk and an autographed copy of the Bible in her desk drawer, Ag thought.

Seemed a waste of time to physically request the certificates with so much available online. But, since Ag was ordering the certificates of another person, not his own or his families' he had to do it in person and show identification.

Apparently, there's a lot of interest in dead person's names and identities these days, Ag thought.

After a long wait, the two certificates were ready and Ag took them to his truck to dissect them.

He took a strong pull on a straw stuck in a plastic tumbler of sweet iced tea and returned it to the cup holder. He wiped his hands on his jeans and pulled out the death certificate of Liam Raymond Nolan. The document was framed with curly black and blue seals and a printed border making it look very official. It was entitled 'Texas Department of Health, Bureau of Vital Statistics'.

"Time of death, location, burial - all as expected," Ag said aloud. "Primary cause of death, blunt force trauma. Other significant conditions, cirrhosis of the liver. No surprise there."

Everything looked as Ag thought it would, so he turned to the birth certificate of Davey Ray Bell. Same fancy scroll around the edges, Seal of the State of Texas, same heading.

"Hmm, born in Llano, Llano County, Texas to Louellen (no middle name) Bell. Male child, DOB, etc. etc. Father listed as 'Unknown'. Similar middle name as Liam, but common in Texas," Ag said to the steering wheel.

He started the truck and left town headed toward Llano.

Merit pressed the intercom on her office phone.

"Val, would you come in please," Merit said into the speaker.

Val came into the office with a legal pad and fancy pen in his hand. He wore a vintage Hugo Boss suit with baby blue bow tie and a modern version of wing tips on his delicate feet.

"Yes ma'am," Val said.

"Nice outfit. I need some help preparing the probate application on Liam Nolan's estate," Merit said.

"Thanks. What do you need for me to do?" Val said.

"Use the forms from the online practice guides for initial filing. Keep it basic for now. You can get the primary info from Liam's files."

"Okay," Val said.

"I want to request that the court appoint me as Executrix and attorney of record since we have the entirety of Liam's records here in the office. Put something in about how the firm was the one he hired and had trusted to sort through the mess. I need to do some research to find out the court rules and where the judge might have some discretion under the circumstances."

"How did you cremate him if the court hasn't appointed you yet?" Val asked.

"No one came forward and it had to be done," Merit said.

"Easier to ask forgiveness than permission?" Val asked.

"Something like that," Merit said.

"Should I add anything about the will that he hadn't signed? His wishes are clearly set out," Val said.

"What a difference three days would have made," Merit said. "Yeah, throw some draft language in there and I'll tweak it."

"Okay."

"You'll need to attach the death certificate that I had Ag pick up at the Bureau of Vital Statistics," Merit said.

"Got it," Val said.

"In the section for identifying heirs, put 'to be determined'. I need to do some research and have Ag check into the possible family that Liam may have missed or ignored," Merit said. "Request letters testamentary. They won't issue them yet, but we might as well put them on notice that we'll be wanting them."

"When do you need it done?"

"I'd like to have it asap. After we get the basic probate petition filed, we can amend later. L.A. Baron says he has an old will. I want to beat him to the courthouse," Merit said. "I don't know his intentions with regard to the estate, but let's not take any chances."

"On it," Val said.

7

Merit walked into her office the next morning and smelled pancakes. Betty came bustling out of the break room.

"Let me guess, Davey is here?" Merit said.

"He said you had a meeting," Betty said.

"In an hour," Merit said. "Guess he came early for breakfast. You know you are training him to show up here any time he's hungry."

"I know, but we can afford to feed him a few meals," Betty said. "Want some pancakes?"

"No thanks. Stuff him full and give me a few minutes," Merit said.

"Softy," Betty smiled at her.

Merit went into her office, unloaded her briefcase and set about organizing her day. When she felt she had control of her priorities, she went into the conference room and found Davey drinking a cup of her coffee. He had a frayed knapsack on the chair beside him.

"Hey, Davey. Did you get enough to eat?"

"Yes, thanks. Betty sure is a good cook," Davey said.

"She is. You should taste her lemon squares with chocolate drizzle," Merit said.

"Really?" Davey licked his lips.

Ag joined them just in time to keep Merit from lecturing Davey about making appointments and eating before he arrived.

The three adjourned to the conference room and sat at the end of a long table. After a few pleasantries, Merit turned to Davey.

"What did you bring for us?" Merit asked.

Davey dumped a big pile of paper and photographs out of a worn backpack and walked over to look out the window. The view was downtown Austin. High rises everywhere and green trees mixed between the water. No wonder everyone loved Austin.

The new skyline had changed so much that Merit barely recognized it. She assumed Davey thought it had always been this way.

Merit turned her eyes to the pile of paper scattered before her.

"What are we looking at here, Davey?" Ag asked.

"Stuff I got from my Mom a while back," Davey said.

Ag began to sort through the stack with a pen letting pages fall away from the center pile. A photograph of a sexy twenty something woman holding a small infant slipped from the edges and Ag pointed to it with the pen. The woman in the picture looked like a young Farrah Fawcett from her days at UT with wing-swept hair and a wide smile. The baby in her arms may have had Liam's eyes.

Hard to tell, Merit thought.

Merit picked up the picture.

"Is this you?" Merit asked.

"Think so," Davey said.

There was a tap at the door and Betty opened it. "Kim Wan is here," she said.

"Show him in, please. And, coffee all around. Tea for me," Merit said.

"I know tea for you," Betty said and stepped back to allow Kim Wan to enter. "Cookies?" Betty asked.

"Yes, please," Davey smiled at her.

By all means, let's work for this kid for free and feed him, too, Merit thought.

An Asian Cajun in a business suit entered the room and pecked Merit on the check. He shook hands with Ag and clapped him on the shoulder.

"Good to see you both," Kim Wan said.

"You too. Kim Wan, this is Davey Bell," Merit said.

Davey turned his attention to the group.

"Davey, this is Kim Wan Thibodeaux. He's the attorney I told you about who does trial law. If it comes to that, he'll be the right person to represent you. If not, he's a good strategist as well and can help in the capacity of negotiation. We work together a lot so he's a friend to the estate."

Davey shyly shook hands and eyed Kim Wan warily. He seemed surprised by the large black freckles on Kim Wan's face. The papulosa had always reminded Merit of Morgan Freeman. Kim Wan was of mixed race, with a Chinese mother and black Cajun father, making him exotic and interesting to look at.

Kim Wan seemed to be sizing up Davey as well.

"I can't afford a lawyer," Davey said to Kim Wan.

"Well, from what Merit has told me it sounds to me like you can't afford not to have one," Kim Wan said.

Davey pulled a purple guitar pick out of this pocket and handed it to Kim Wan.

"This is important to me. It was Liam's. If you'll take it for now, I'll pay you when I can."

"Merit made me aware of your situation. For now, I'll keep abreast of what's developing with the estate and we'll discuss moving forward if something is required to be filed in court," Kim Wan said. "You hang onto that guitar pick. You might need it."

"Let's go through the rest of this information you brought in," Merit said to Davey.

All four sat at the conference table and began to make small stacks from the backpack dump.

"Would you put these pictures in order as best you can by the age of the infant - which we assume is you," Merit said.

"I'll sort through the letters," Ag said.

"I've got the legal documents," Kim Wan said.

"I'll take the notes and the miscellaneous," Merit said.

All four heads bowed as they worked and catalogued the material.

"I have the pictures in order, and I put sticky notes with my best guess of the dates on the back," Davey said.

"There's nothing in the legal docs that pertain to Liam Nolan as far as I can tell," Kim Wan said.

"Here is a lot of correspondence with various music groups from around the time Davey was born. A couple of them have the initial 'L'. Could be Liam," Ag said.

"I'll ask Val if Liam ever used an 'L' like that in his file documents," Merit said.

"I'll send over a copy of Davey's birth certificate," Ag said to Kim Wan. "Doesn't show much."

"How did you get my birth certificate?" Davey said.

"It's public record, son," Ag said.

"I need more time with the notes, but I think we have a rough idea of what's here," Merit said. "I'll have Val do a timeline and compare it to the timeline he's doing with Liam's estate files. We'll see if anything matches up. Maybe he was in Llano, maybe not."

"There's a lot here, but none of it appears conclusive so far," Kim Wan said. "Did your mother ever tell you who your father was?"

"No, she almost told me once, but she changed her mind and wouldn't say," Davey said.

"Was she ever married?" Merit asked.

"Yeah. There were a lot of men around," Davey said.

"I don't want to cause you pain, Davey, but it might be helpful if we were able to talk to her," Merit said.

"I've never been able to locate her when I've needed her before. I just learned to stop needing her," Davey said.

"Where did she last live?" Ag asked.

"Her parents left her a house in Llano. We lived there for a while when I was small. I don't know if she sold it," Davey said.

"Is this the house?" Merit asked showing Davey another photo with a swing set in the back yard.

"Looks like it," Davey said. "It's hard to remember."

"Ag, see what you can dig up," Merit said.

"On my list," Ag said.

"I think it's time we did a DNA test to find out who you are," Merit said to Davey.

"As I said, I can't afford that, and I don't have anything of Liam's to use for a test," Davey said.

"As we discussed, I think I can have the estate pay for the test, and the county coroner will have DNA because the homicide is unsolved," Merit said.

Davey flinched.

"I know this is tough, but we need to get the facts straight so Merit can proceed with sorting things out in probate court," Kim Wan said.

Davey took a deep breath.

"What if my blood test shows up something else? Will you give it to the police?" Davey asked.

Merit and Ag shared a look.

"That's not our intention, but once it's done, we may not be able to keep the police from obtaining it in the future," Merit said. "The probate court will have access to the DNA report and probate records are public."

"What are you trying to hide?" Kim Wan asked.

"Nothing, you just can't be too careful anymore," Davey said.

"Davey, is there something we should talk about in private before you make this decision? We can step out and find an empty office." Kim Wan said.

"No, no, I guess not," Davey said.

"It's your call. Do you want to establish paternity or do you want to protect your right to privacy?" Merit said.

Kim Wan, Ag, and Merit all looked at Davey's sweet face and waited for his answer.

"I want to know if Liam was my father. Let's do it," Davey said. "I need to know where I come from."

"We'll keep it as quiet as possible." Merit nodded at Ag.

"I'll set it up," Ag said. "Call me tomorrow at the number on this card."

After Davey left, Merit, Ag, and Kim Wan looked at each other across the conference table.

"What are we getting into here?" Merit asked.

"My thoughts exactly," Kim Wan said. "I think this kid might need protection, but if he won't come clean, I can't help him."

"What if we do the paternity test through your office and ask for reimbursement later if we need it in probate court," Merit said. "That way, no one will know about Davey until we're ready to reveal his status, if any."

"I think that's a good idea," Kim Wan said. "How can you get DNA material without setting off suspicion at the coroner's office?"

"I've got friends over there. I'll see if I can get a bit of blood or hair," Ag said.

"Can you keep your friend from knowing why you need it?" Merit asked.

"I'll try. I'll use a number ID for both Liam and Davey instead of their names when we run the test," Ag said.

All three nodded.

♪

Merit stayed late at the office to have some quiet time for research.

"Let's see who gets all these music rights and songs since Liam didn't have a will?" she said to the black computer screen.

She fired up her computer and clicked into the Texas Estates Code, Title 2, Subtitle E, the statutes covering intestate succession and the law of descent and distribution.

Next, she went through the court cases on intestate succession in Texas and the rest of the Southern District. She remembered a little from her law school wills and estates class, and she'd had a few cases in her law practice that touched on the subject, but she wanted to refresh her memory and dig into the nitty-gritty of the law. Too bad Liam had died without signing his new will. Intestate succession was a messy procedure and never quite tied up all the loose ends. She knew that an heir could come out of the woodwork years later and cause trouble even after the court had signed off and the assets had been distributed.

First Merit scrolled through the cases on those dying without a will who were married. In that case, the surviving spouse would inherit all the property of the marriage and one-third of Liam's separate property. Separate property was listed as assets owned before the marriage, or after a divorce.

"Check that one off for now. No spouse that we know of."

Merit took a quick look at the statute when parents were alive or there were brothers and sisters. Liam was unmarried, his parents were dead, and he had no siblings that could be identified.

"Check that one off too. No living parents or brothers and sisters."

Merit moved on to the instance where there were children, but no current spouse or parents alive. In that case, if Davey was proved to be Liam's son, Davey would inherit everything. It would be up to Davey if he wanted to honor any of Liam's last wishes or whether Davey would devise an entirely new plan based on his preferences.

If Davey was not Liam's son, and Ag located no other missing heirs, the property would escheat into the State of Texas coffers. This rarely happened, as the laws were designed to get property to anyone who was even remotely related to the deceased.

Maybe Ag will find something or someone. I don't know if that would be good or bad, Merit thought.

8

L.A. Baron sat in his Austin office in the downtown warehouse district high above the restaurants, bars, and traffic that made up Austin's hottest new business sector researching the same celebrity probates that Merit was reviewing. His office was almost a duplicate of his Los Angeles digs, modern, cold and impersonal. A first-rate music system was on the shelves mounted on one wall. Stacks of demo CD's and flash drives were located beside it. There was also a duplicate black door in the far corner marked *PRIVATE* with a similar metal keypad by the door handle.

L.A. preferred to spend his time in Los Angeles, but felt one must keep up appearances in Austin, the Live Music Capital of the World. He looked down on all the little people walking around during lunch hour. He dialed up his local counsel's office and spoke into the microphone on his desk phone.

"L.A. Baron for Richard Rooter."

L.A. drummed his fingers on his desk as he waited to be connected.

"What can I do for you L.A.?" The voice of Richard 'Scooter' Rooter said over the speaker.

"I want to hire the meanest litigator in Austin who also knows about wills and estates. Merit Bridges is about to get a wake-up call," L.A. said.

"Rightly so. I can see why you are upset," Rooter said. "She's taken over."

"Who does she think she is to rule over his memorial? She's not even in the will. There is no will. I should have taken over that service and showed her who's in charge right up front," L.A. said. "I'm going to petition the court to appoint me as executor instead of Merit Bridges."

"Appearances are important, but it's the probate court judge who'll decide who's in charge," Rooter said.

"Yeah, but her picture is online and in all the papers with the urn," L.A. said.

"Missed opportunity. There will be others," Rooter said.

"Do some research and get me some names of good estate lawyers," L.A. said.

"You'll need someone who has some street cred with the probate courts," Rooter said.

"Find one and make it a man. I don't need any more estrogen around me right now," L.A. said.

"I already know the right guy. I'll check and see if he's available. But, the courts are reluctant to swap out executors unless there's a good reason."

"You let me worry about that. Just find me a lawyer ASAP," L.A. said.

"You got it," Rooter said.

L.A. hung up the phone and faced the entourage sitting around the room on leather sofas and chairs with glass tables mixed between. The minions all waited silently for the next command.

How can I get this estate away from her? I'm not about to let some Texas lawyer get one up on me, L.A. thought.

The minions stared at L.A.

"I want to know everyone Liam talked to or worked with in the last year," L.A. said.

"What up?" Minion One said. "Liam was a worthless bum."

"You don't need to know what up yet," L.A. said. "Just do what I tell you."

"You got it, L.A.," Ash said. "I've been watching *Fever Stomp* in Japan. You think it's going viral, don't you?"

"A new song is going viral?" Minion Two asked.

L.A. gave Ash a foul look that said, "Keep your mouth shut."

9

M erit sat at her desk and clicked through some historical news sources online and in the various bar journals around the country.

James Brown, Jerry Garcia, and Michael Jackson were the source of the most famous music related estate battles.

James Brown, "The Godfather of Soul," died of heart failure in late 2006 at age 73. He left an estate of about $100 million. His will said that he wanted his money to be divided between two trusts: one for the education of his grandchildren and one for the education of the needy children living in Georgia and South Carolina.

Brown's will contained a familiar clause that stated if he failed to provide for any relatives that the failure was intentional and not an accident or mistake. Regardless of the clause, Brown's wife and children challenged the will and were awarded half of his fortune by the court.

Later, a record producer who had helped Brown start the original trusts for the nonprofits challenged the decision. She asserted that the trusts were his last wish and that she was to administer the nonprofits after his death.

"*Get On Up*. Greed rules," Merit said.

She clicked around through the other sites and found information about Jerry Garcia's estate. Garcia, the front man for the Grateful Dead left about $7 million. Several sued for the money including an ex-wife, his daughter, and his widow. Seems the ex-wife got about $5 million to fulfill an old divorce settlement. The remainder of the heirs divided the rest of the money, but the fight went on for the so-called Garcia Tapes of unreleased music.

"*Ripple*," Merit said.

Finally, she looked at the big kahuna, the estate of Michael Jackson. The main issue there was who would get custody of the singer's three children. The battle turned on keeping the children away from the pop star's abusive father, Joe Jackson. It had been documented that the father would beat Michael and the other Jackson children with whatever he could get his hands on, including electrical cords from irons. He would also throw the children up against the wall as hard as he could.

In his will, Michael Jackson left custody of all three children to their grandmother, Katherine Jackson. Debbie Rowe, the mother of the two elder children, but not Blanket, could have asked for custody, but seems she settled with Katherine for extra visitation and who knows what else. Money was certainly involved even though she had already received a hefty settlement when she and Michael Jackson divorced in 1999. Even so, Rowe had a strong claim to custody, being the children's mother.

Of course, whomever got the kiddos got the estate money to manage. So even though the will was valid, there was plenty of battle ground left to fight for control of the kids.

"Nothing is *Black or White*," Merit said.

Merit found that the most famous case of intestate succession was the Howard Hughes Estate case out of Houston. Merit's mentor, Woodward 'Woody' Preston had worked on that case when he was a young lawyer. He'd told Merit numerous stories about it. She clicked on the speaker and speed dialed Woody's home number. Hearing his familiar voice answer the phone sent a wave of peace over Merit. He never failed to comfort her or brighten her day. He had long ago forgiven her for accidentally putting him in the path of a maniac and almost getting him killed in a wild ride through River Oaks in Houston.

"It's good to hear your voice," Woody said. "How's Ace doing?"

"Fine. He'll be home this weekend. You should run by and spy on him for me," Merit laughed.

"I've been thinking of just that. Maybe lunch next with the young lad," Woody said.

"Have time for a lawyerly chat?" Merit asked.

"Always with you," Woody said.

"I've got a probate case without a will. A young man is claiming heirship and I've ordered DNA. Assuming the kiddo belongs to the deceased, what can you tell me about intestate succession?" Merit asked.

"As you probably know, if you prove the young man is the deceased's heir, he will inherit everything. If there is no heir, and the deceased had his domicile in Texas, then the State will grab the funds and hold onto them for about seven years. If no one shows up to claim the assets, they escheat to the state.

"I found a case where the state took the funds and put them into the general account. No way to designate where the funds would be spent," Merit said.

"That's the gist of it. If no one claims the money, the state can spend it anywhere they like," Woody said.

"So much for giving it all to music and the arts," Merit said.

"Was that Liam's last wish?" Woody asked.

"Yes. He was planning to set up a foundation as soon as Val completed the inventory. There wasn't a lot of value left, but Liam wanted to help where he could," Merit said.

"Admirable. It's a shame," Woody said.

"Tell me again about the Dummar will trial," Merit said.

"I worked on that case for years," Woody said.

"I love your war stories," Merit said.

"Melvin Dummar had apparently picked up a bum in a Nevada dessert who turned out to be the late Howard Hughes. Dummar said he'd been given a handwritten will by Hughes and tried to probate it. When the firm and I went to court, we disproved the will using large trial exhibits. The words were copied from various memos and letters written by Hughes before his death. The handwriting samples from Hughes' spelling out: 'THIS IS NOT MY WILL.'"

"Just like Perry Mason would have done it," Merit said.

"Very effective, since we ultimately won and disproved the claim." Woody said.

"That story will be told for generations," Merit said.

"Rumors still circulate that the will was valid and Dummar had been screwed by the system," Woody said.

"Is it true?" Merit asked.

"Doubtful, but I guess we'll never really know," Woody said.

"Legendary," Merit said.

"Distant relatives of Hughes split up what was left of the estate after the executor and lawyers stretched out the case for years and took their cut. That was after my involvement," Woody said.

"There has to be a cousin or distant relative of Liam out there somewhere," Merit said.

"Nothing says that person, if found, would use the money in the way Liam would have wanted," Woody said.

"True. So very true," Merit said.

They rang off and Merit tidied up to leave for the day. When the DNA tests were complete, Merit would probably know where the money was going. Would Liam have been happy to have a son? Did he know? Had he denied Davey? Would he have changed his plans for a son he'd never known? There was no way to be sure.

"If Davey is Liam's son, I just hope the kid doesn't blow it all in a month, or worse, spend it all on drugs and kill himself," Merit said out loud.

10

L.A. and his attorney, Thomas Tipton, entered Travis County Probate Court Number 1 in the Travis County Courthouse on Guadalupe Street in downtown Austin.

They walked into the chamber, a bustling room full of attorneys and clients, in line on the regular docket.

When their case was called L.A. and Tipton positioned themselves at the Petitioner's table and waited for the circus to begin. Merit took her position behind the Respondent's table and watched them whisper behind their hands. Merit's office staff sat behind her in a line of support like birds on a wire waiting to swoop in and prop her up if needed.

L.A. looked over at Merit and smirked. Her armpits prickled so strongly she felt an electric shock. She turned her head toward Val and pretended not to notice.

What is this guy's beef with me? Merit thought.

After the initial courtroom rituals, Judge Madeline Herman got down to business. She was a round middle aged woman who took no guff. She sat on the judge's throne like a giant hen guarding eggs in a nest.

"This is a hearing on the matter of the Executor of the Estate of Liam Raymond Nolan," Judge Herman said.

"Please proceed, Mr. Tipton."

"The petitioner, Mr. Baron, requests that he be appointed executor of the estate of Liam Nolan. My client Mr. Baron is uniquely positioned to serve the estate as he is currently managing part of the portfolio of Mr. Nolan under a contract with him in both local and Los Angeles offices. He has a unique knowledge of the music industry."

"Ms. Bridges?" Judge Herman said.

"Your Honor," Merit said. "Liam Nolan was a client of my firm at the time of his death. He made his final wishes known to me, and our office was in the process of drafting a will and trust for him when he died."

"This may be true, Your Honor," said Mr. Tipton, "but circumstances have changed and it's in the best interest of the estate to appoint my client. He has a law degree as well."

Merit looked at Val and he handed her a file with several copies of documents inside.

"As you can see from this correspondence, Your Honor, Mr. Nolan severed his contract with Mr. Baron several years ago. His only attachment to Mr. Baron's company at the time of his death was a management contract that was held in play by royalties still being paid out on old arrangements. When those run out, Mr. Baron will have nothing further to manage. Liam Nolan asserted to me that he would not be doing business with Mr. Baron again."

"Objection, Your Honor," Tipton said. "There's no proof of the origin of these documents."

"One moment," Judge Herman said. She took the folder, opened it with a hand adorned by long red fake fingernails, and studied the documents contained there.

"Mr. Baron, did you ever receive this correspondence from Mr. Nolan informing you that your services would not be needed after his contract ran out?" Judge Herman asked.

"Not to my knowledge," L.A. said.

"May I assert further, Your Honor, that most of Mr. Nolan's possessions of any value, except for his guitars, are housed in my office. He rented a very small furnished studio with few personal belongings when he passed," Merit said.

"Understood," Judge Herman said. "For now, let's let Ms. Bridges continue to unwind the estate. She has a history with the court and on its face the decedent was comfortable with her as his representative. Your rights will be fully protected by the court, Mr. Baron."

Merit smiled at the judge.

"We'll see about that," L.A. whispered to Tipton.

After losing at the probate hearing, L.A. was in a foul mood. He shooed the minions from his office and Ash, the last one out, closed the outer door. L.A. locked it behind them.

He put his mobile phone on the desk and walked to the opposite corner of the room to the small closet door marked PRIVATE. He unlocked the door with the keypad, looked inside, allowing his eyes to adjust to the dark, and walked into the four feet by six feet chamber. He pulled the door toward him and locked it with a slide which shoved a four-inch bolt into place with a thunk.

L.A. sat on a hard stool positioned in the middle of the floor, the only item in the room. He sat for some time in the sound proof chamber. No one outside the room would know what occurred inside.

11

Ag entered the Austin Police Department, went through the metal detector, checked his gun in the small lockers at the entrance, and asked the receptionist if Detective Chaplain was in.

"Take a seat and I'll check," the cute young receptionist gushed at Ag from behind a bullet proof glass with a microphone at chin level. The flirting, as usual, was lost on him, as he'd never been one to think of himself as attractive or much of a catch to women.

Ag only had a minute to wait. Chaplain came out, clapped Ag on the shoulder, and shook his hand. Chaplain's full head of hair made him look younger than he was. His name plate didn't have his first name, as everyone just called the detective Chaplain. It had become an honorary moniker as well as his last name.

"How the hell are ya'? I wondered when I'd be hearing from you on this case," Chaplain said.

"I'm good. You? What case?" Ag laughed.

"We saw you with Merit Bridges at the funeral and assumed you'd be working the Nolan estate with her," Chaplain said.

"Well, since the cat's out of the bag, any progress on the murder?" Ag said. "Buzz around town is that his death was a mugging."

"We thought so at first, but the rage was pretty severe for a snatch and grab. Medical examiner says the perp continued to beat

Nolan after he was down and unable to fight back. Also, nothing was missing from the body as far as we could tell."

"So you've changed your theory of the crime," Ag said.

"Only his guitar case was gone, and since that was the murder weapon, we're pretty sure it was not a mugging."

"Do you know who might have killed him?" Ag asked.

We've got a suspect," Chaplain said.

"Anyone I know?" Ag asked.

"What do you know about a kid named Davey Ray Bell?" Chaplain said.

"Nothing I can share," Ag said. "Certainly, nothing pertaining to the murder,"

"Word on the street is he was following Nolan around. Stalking comes to mind," Chaplain said.

"Stalking?" Ag said. "Have you ever met Davey Bell? He looks like a wholesome commercial for drinking milk. Except for his dirty hair."

"Not yet. I'm having him brought in for questioning this afternoon," Chaplain said.

♪

Merit saw Ag settle into a corner table at Eastside Cafe as she walked in wearing a black pencil skirt showing just the right amount of leg and a silky sleeveless top in a jeweled blue color. She had an equestrian print Hermes scarf tied around the handle of her Louis Vuitton tote bag. Blue was Ag's favorite color, after Aggie maroon, of course.

Ag dropped his napkin as Merit gave him her best smile. She noticed him fidget as he stood, pulled out her chair and seated her.

"Howdy," Merit said.

"Howdy to you," Ag said. "You look great in that color."

"Thank you, sir. What's for lunch?" Merit smiled.

She avoided any further eye contact by opening the menu and looked up when the waitress arrived.

"Specials today are on the right side. You may know we grow most of our own vegetables, and our eggs are from our free-range hens."

"We're regulars," Ag said.

"Drinks?" the waitress asked.

"Unsweet tea," Merit said.

"Sweet tea," Ag said.

"Ready to order?" the waitress asked.

Ag nodded to Merit.

"I'll have the mushroom crepes," Merit said.

"Sesame catfish," Ag said.

The waitress hustled off to get the order in ahead of the gathering crowd.

"Yum!" Merit said. "I'm starved."

"No wine today?" Ag asked.

"Busy afternoon. Betty has me catching up on correspondence. Ugh!" Merit said.

"You called this meeting. What's up?" Ag said.

"Well, first, I haven't seen you alone since the festival and I wanted to thank you for donating your time to run security. Lunch is my treat."

"You're welcome," Ag said.

Second, I'd like for you to go to Llano and see what you can dig up on Davey and his mother while we wait for the results of the paternity test," Merit said.

"I can go first thing tomorrow. What am I looking for, the usual or something special?" Ag asked.

"Here's a list Val prepped of the hill country venues where Liam might have played music around the time Davey was born. It's in order time-wise as best he could calculate from the dates of Liam's tours and albums."

Merit handed Ag a thin manila folder with 'Nolan, Liam - Timeline' written on the tab in Val's beautiful script.

"I guess it's best to just use your gut and see if any red flags come up. Also, check the court records under Louellen Bell, Davey's mother, for marriage licenses and divorces from about twenty years ago through current date," Merit said.

"Does Davey's mother still live there?" Ag asked.

"Not sure. Davey says his Grandmother lived in Llano her entire life so Louellen Bell should either be there now or have a trail of some sort over there," Merit said. "See if you can find the family home if it exists. Davey didn't know if Louellen still owned it."

"When was the last time he spoke with her?" Ag asked.

"He says it's been years. She's basically abandoned him to fend for himself. Imagine not knowing where your mother is," Merit said.

"I'll get over to Llano right away. Verbal or written report?" Ag asked.

"Give me a call if you find something earth shaking. Otherwise a report in a few days is fine."

"And if I find Louellen Bell?"

"I don't know if that would be good news or bad news," Merit said. "Not exactly the mother of the year."

They paused while the waitress served their food.

"Looks great!" both said at the same time and laughed.

After the waitress departed, Ag said, "Speaking of bad news, I met with Detective Chaplain this morning. Did you get my message?"

"Yes. I got it walking out the door, but I knew I was about to see you so I haven't listened yet. What happened?" Merit asked from behind her napkin that was hiding her mouth full of food.

"I think he suspects Davey Bell of having something to do with Liam's death. He's bringing Davey in for questioning this afternoon," Ag said.

"Oh no. I wonder if Davey informed Kim Wan. It would be just like that kid to go in there alone," Merit said and reached into her bag for her phone.

♪

That evening, Kim Wan and Merit met in her office for a recap and a nightcap.

"Looks like APD has drone footage of Davey lurking around Liam on the night of the murder," Kim Wan said.

"How did they get drone footage?" Merit asked.

"It's in the cloud, on shared public websites and social media pages, everywhere," Kim Wan said.

"These drones have become like mosquitos," Merit said.

"I even had a client bring drugs across the border with a drone. Dropped the dope right into the valley for months before border patrol caught on," Kim Wan said.

"I had no idea they were so handy," Merit said.

"Later, after he was convicted, the same client had cell phones dropped into prison with drones. He got caught there, too," Kim Wan said.

"Repeat business," Merit said.

"In Davey's case, a couple of teenagers were on the lake taking pictures at first light with their drones. They later uploaded the footage to some teenage website. Two bicycle cops stopped them and questioned them. They saw Liam down there. The cops remembered the drone cameras and advised APD. The teens responded to a request for information on local news and brought in their photos," Kim Wan said.

"How do you establish chain of custody with something like that? What about redacting data outside of a warrant?" Merit asked. "Anyone could have cut whatever they wanted from the evidence."

"Probably can't establish custody from start to finish. Hobbyists are supposed to register their drones on the FAA website, so it's not that difficult to find amateur drone enthusiasts if they follow the rules. Wouldn't matter in this case. The footage may not be admissible, but it pointed APD toward Davey and they found security camera footage of him and pieced their case together. Using security camera footage, it's easy to establish chain of custody since the city owns the cameras. It set the dominoes falling," Kim Wan said.

"Is there a lot of footage of Davey hanging out around Liam?" Merit asked.

"Enough," Kim Wan said.

"All circumstantial evidence," Merit said. "These are inconvenient facts, but they don't mean he's guilty."

"Right, but there's plenty of other evidence pointing at Davey. Enough for the grand jury to indict," Kim Wan said. "And, the flyer sees what the drone sees, so the teenager can testify as to what he was watching at the time the photos were taken. In this case, that won't be necessary and the teenagers were probably stoned anyway."

"What about privacy?" Merit asked.

"It's up to each state, but the rules aren't uniform and they aren't clear. It's a whole new field of law and evidence," Kim Wan said. "And, we can argue that it's natural for Davey to want to find out about a man who he thought was his father."

"They could turn that around and say it's reason to kill him as well," Merit said.

"That's right. If he's charged, I'll have to find a way to rebut that," Kim Wan said.

"Still, they don't have Davey on tape committing the murder. And, no fingerprints," Merit said.

"True. It will be hard to convict without a smoking gun," Kim Wan said.

"Or smoking guitar in this case," Merit said. "It's almost funny."

"Yes, but it's not," Kim Wan said.

"Maybe a little funny," Merit said.

12

Merit and Betty sat in Merit's office watching the evening news before going home for the day. Val, the receptionist Mai, and the other interns had already left and the office was quiet with most of the machines turned off. Merit sipped a glass of spicy Texas Legato Tempranillo while Betty had her once a week whiskey. Today's selection was Swift's Single Malt out of Dripping Springs.

They watched Red Thallon, reporting the news on KNEW. She'd given them some good press on one of their former cases. Red had also heroically foiled a former boy toy of Merit's who'd spied on her for a story. She had also been the primary reporter at the charity music fest.

Red stood in front of APD with microphone in perfectly manicured hand. She had on her signature short skirt with lots of tanning-bed colored skin glistening in the sunshine. Her red hair was pulled back with a leather string but a few strands still managed to sneak out and blow around in the wind.

"Davey Ray Bell has been arrested for the murder of Liam Nolan. He has been a suspect in the case for some time according to APD sources. Bell allegedly stalked Nolan for several months and was seen on several drone video recordings watching him and attempting to speak with him," Red reported.

Merits armpits prickled. "Could we be mistaken about him?" she asked Betty.

"I don't think so," Betty said. "That poor child is in a world of hurt."

"Yes. But I guess anyone could do anything on a given day," Merit said.

On screen Red continued, "Check Austin9Online for further details and updates throughout the day."

The phone rang on Merit's desk and Betty punched the speaker button.

"Law office of Merit Bridges," Betty said.

"Betty, this is Kim Wan for Merit," the speaker reported.

"Hi, Kim Wan. I'm here. You're on speaker," Merit said. "We're watching it now."

"If you're clear with the estate and protection from the conflict of interest, I hope we can accelerate the DNA test and maybe show Davey had a reason to be around Liam," Kim Wan said.

"As we discussed, that could be misconstrued, couldn't it?" Merit asked.

"How so?" Betty asked.

"Davey's anger at not having a father could be interpreted as a motive," Merit said.

"I'd like to know either way," Kim Wan said.

"After we get the results, we can keep it quiet for now and release it later when we're ready," Merit said.

"Good idea," Kim Wan said.

"We should see if Ag can rush up the test results. You want to call him or do you want me to?" Merit asked.

"Why don't you do it? He likes you more than me," Kim Wan said.

"Yeah, right. Later," Merit said and hung up.

Betty picked up her drink, took a long pull, and turned to Merit.

"You never get all your coons up the tree at the same time, do you?"

Merit looked at Davey's picture on the TV screen.

"Who's your daddy?"

The next day Merit sat behind her desk, looked out the window at downtown Austin and sipped hot tea. Ag entered Merit's office with a cup of coffee in hand and sat in one of the two guest chairs in front of Merit's desk. Betty came in behind him but didn't speak.

"Well, what?" Merit asked.

"The DNA results are in," Ag said.

"I'm stayin'," Betty said and sat down in the other guest chair.

Ag handed Merit a brown envelope with a large number 732 stamped on the outside in red.

"Anonymous ID number?" Merit asked.

"Yep," Ag said.

Merit turned the envelope over and saw that it was still clasped and glued shut.

"You didn't open it?" Merit asked.

"Thought you'd want to do the honors," Ag said.

Merit pulled open her desk drawer and took out a Waterford letter opener that her deceased husband, Tony, had given her many Christmases ago. She slit the end of the envelope and placed the opener on the desk. She pulled out two sheets of letter-sized paper and scanned the pages.

"It's a boy!" Merit said.

"Thought so," Ag said.

"I'll call Kim Wan," Merit said.

"Poor Liam," Betty said. "He finally has a family and it's too late."

13

Merit and Kim Wan went into the Travis County Jail and signed in to see Davey Ray Bell. When they were settled into a small drab interview room, Davey was brought in wearing an orange jump suit that made him look like a skinny pumpkin. He looked so sad Merit could not speak for a moment.

"Hey," Davey said.

"Hi, Davey," Merit said. "How are you holding up?"

"Not so great," Davey said.

"Have you been mistreated?" Kim Wan asked.

"Other than being in jail?" Davey asked.

"I understand. I'll do my best to get you out of here," Kim Wan said. "We'll discuss all that when Merit leaves. For now, she has something to tell you."

Davey looked at Merit with dread in his eyes.

"What now?" Davey asked.

"I've received the results of the paternity test," Merit said.

Davey looked at Merit as though he could not take another disappointment or any news of consequence.

"Liam was your father," Merit said.

"Father. Mine. What?" Davey asked then burst into tears.

Merit fumbled in her purse for a tissue and handed it to him.

"Do you need a minute?" Merit asked.

Davey blew his nose then took a breath.

"No, I'm okay I guess. I was half expecting it, but it's still a shock," Davey said.

"Listen up. Now that we can file the documents with the court about your heirship to Liam's estate, there are a few things I need to tell you," Merit said.

"Is it good news or bad news?" Davey asked.

"First, I'm going to wait a while before I file the paternity results, so keep it to yourself for now," Merit said.

"I will," Davey said.

"Second, there's a man in the record business based out of Los Angeles. He has an office just down the street in the Warehouse District. His name is L.A. Baron," Merit said.

"L.A. from L.A.?" Davey asked.

"Right, he worked with your father years back," Merit said.

"My father? That sounds so strange," Davey said.

"It must. It will take some time to adjust. What I want you to know is that L.A. Baron has filed a motion to be appointed as executor of the estate. It would not change your right to inherit, now that paternity has been established. But it would give him control of how the money is doled out, when, and where any income would be reinvested, that type of thing," Merit said.

"I thought you were in charge of the estate. You won't let him have control, will you?" Davey asked.

"Not if I can help it. The court should stick with me since I have all the background from the estate planning with your father," Merit said.

"My father," Davey said.

"It will grow on you," Kim Wan said.

"Why does this L.A. guy care about the estate?" Davey asked.

"I'm not sure. It seems a lot of work for little return. He does have a few songs and lyric copyrights left under an old management contract with Liam, but it's not worth a lot to someone like L.A. Baron," Merit said.

"How much would he get if he took over the estate?" Davey said.

"It's usually a percentage of the overall value, usually paid per year until the funds are distributed to heirs or a trust or whatever is relevant to the particular estate. All subject to court approval, of course. That's why I don't see his interest. It's a lot of work for a small percentage," Merit said.

"He's already getting a percentage for management. How greedy can he be?" Davey said.

"Oh, my naive dear. You have no idea what can happen when power and money get into someone's blood. Even estates as small as Liam's can become a battleground," Merit said.

The next afternoon Betty's voice came over the speaker on Merit's desk.

"Merit, it's Redmond Thallon at KNEW. She says she needs to speak to you right away."

"Thanks, put her through," Merit said.

Merit hit the speaker button, got up, and closed her door.

"Hey Red," Merit called out as she walked back to her desk.

"Merit, I'm calling officially to give you a chance to comment on a story. I'm airing it on the six o'clock news. Unofficially, I'm giving you a head's up about your Liam Nolan estate and his heirs," Red said.

"Go on," Merit said.

"I have the DNA test results showing the paternity of Liam Raymond Nolan as the father of Davey Ray Bell," Red said.

Merit pulled the file with the DNA results from her desk drawer and looked inside. It was still there.

"How did you obtain that information?" Merit asked.

"You know I can't tell you, but in this case, I don't know. It was sent in an email and we confirmed the story with APD," Red said.

"So, assuming it's true, Detective Chaplain knows too?" Merit asked.

"Apparently."

"How? How could anyone know this?" Merit said out loud.

"Do you want to make a comment, or try to get out ahead of this?" Red asked.

"What's in it for you?" Merit asked.

"Confirm the email is not a fake and give me an exclusive," Red said.

"Hold on a second," Merit said and pressed the mute button on the phone.

Merit did a quick mental inventory of who knew about the test results. Betty, Ag, and Val were bullet proof when it came to confidentiality. Kim Wan was trustworthy as well, and he said he hadn't shared the information with his staff. The lab could not have known who the parties were because of the blind numbering system Ag had used.

How could anyone know? What purpose would they have in revealing it to the press and APD? Merit thought.

She pondered the situation for another full minute then pressed the mute off button.

"Can you meet me at the probate court in one hour? If you give me that much time, I'll give you the exclusive and a brief on-camera soundbite," Merit said.

"Done. See you there," Red said.

Merit and Val walked over to the probate court with a copy of the amended petition in hand advising the court of the DNA results. Merit had filed the amendment electronically per Travis County requirements, but wanted to have a prop for talking with the press and a copy for Red. Kim Wan was there waiting for them.

Red was already set up on the courthouse steps with the KNEW van out front. Val stepped behind the cameraman to watch and Merit walked up the steps and stood beside the reporter.

"We'll just cut this into what's already been shot. Ready?" Red asked.

"Let's do it," Merit answered.

Val gave Merit a reassuring smile, held two thumbs up and mouthed, "You look great!"

Red, apparently assuming the compliment was for her, mouthed, "Thanks."

Val rolled his eyes at Merit. Merit laughed a bit and relaxed.

"Merit Bridges is here today with a KNEW exclusive regarding the murder and probate of the estate of musician Liam Nolan. Ms. Bridges, as attorney for the estate of the deceased, what can you tell us?" Red said into the camera. She turned to Merit and moved the microphone to Merit's mouth.

Merit handed the amendment to Red.

"We have just filed an amendment to the petition for probate after receiving the results of a paternity test. It proves that Davey Ray Bell is Liam Nolan's natural son."

"Did Davey Bell kill Liam Nolan to inherit from his estate?" Red asked.

"The estate is modest and I doubt anyone would kill for it, least of all Davey Bell. That said, I have no information regarding his culpability one way or the other," Merit said knowing that she was to appear unbiased in her role as executrix.

"Is it true that Davey Bell is homeless and lives on the street?" Red asked.

"I only know that he has no permanent residence at the present time. There have been many unfortunate events in his life. I'm glad he now knows who his father is and can own his heritage," Merit said.

"You heard it here, Austin!" Red said to the camera and made a cutting gesture across her throat.

"Thanks, Merit," Red said and extended her hand. Merit shook it warmly.

"When did Chaplain get the results? Before or after he arrested Davey Bell? If you know," Merit said.

"The word out is that it was before. It's one of the reasons Bell was charged," Red said.

"I hate to think we helped put that boy in jail. Off the record," Merit said.

"Of course," Red said.

"Thanks for giving me a chance to file this first," Merit said.

"I hate to be the one to tell you, but the email said there's more," Red said.

"More? How? What's next?" Merit said.

Merit called Betty in first thing the next morning.

"Did you see the news report?" Merit asked.

"Yes. Nice that Red allowed you to make your comments ahead of the release of the story," Betty said.

"Agreed. But, how did someone get the results of the test before we filed it with the probate court?" Merit asked.

"I was wondering that myself," Betty said.

"Maybe a slip up somewhere, but let's have this place de-bugged, just in case," Merit said.

"Right away," Betty said.

"Notify Ag too, please," Merit said.

Betty started to say something. Appeared to think better of it, and said, "Right away.

L.A. watched the KNEW daily news from his chrome and glass desk in his downtown Austin office. All three minions were present and sucking up to him at a record high.

"I like the looks of Ms. Red Thallon," Minion One said.

"Like you stand a chance with her," Minion Two said.

Ash gave them both an admonishing look.

"What?" Minion One asked.

"Quiet, I can't hear," L.A. said.

Red was onscreen with the full presentation of the story that featured the DNA report and Merit Bridges. A commercial replaced the news feed.

"Looks like that took them off guard," Ash said. "I bet they're scratching their heads about how that DNA info got out."

"Just the beginning," L.A. said.

14

Merit and Kim Wan entered Criminal Court Number Three of the Travis County Courthouse. Kim Wan, all business, proceeded to the defense table and Merit quietly slipped into a seat at the back of the room.

Ash Joyner, L.A.'s third minion, sat on the other side of the aisle wearing a cap pulled low and holding a miniature tape recorder that he was hiding under a copy of *The Austin Chronicle*. He appeared to be reading the ads for local venues featuring live music over the upcoming weekend. He circled with a red pen an all female show featuring Toni Price, Lou Ann Barton, Nanci Griffith and Sara Hickman at the Continental Club later that night. In the margin on the side of the paper, he kept a running account of the time and what was occurring in the courtroom.

The prisoners on the day's docket were brought into a holding area beside the jury box which was empty. Merit saw Davey in the group. He nodded to Kim Wan then looked around the room until he locked eyes with her. Davey looked miserable and even thinner, if that was possible, but in one piece and undamaged.

Judge Crow, in monochromatic black, and looking stern took the bench and called the room to order.

The once muscular bailiff in a uniform two sizes too small stepped up to the front and addressed the court. "We have eighteen prisoners here for arraignment and bail hearings today, Your Honor,"

"Proceed," Judge Crow said.

After a few arraignments were handled, the bailiff brought Davey to the defense table in handcuffs.

The prosecutor stepped up to the front of the room and after a nod from the judge said, "We request no bail in this case. For all intents and purposes, the accused is homeless, has no ties to the community, and is a college dropout."

"Defense?" Judge Crow asked.

"Your Honor, Davey Bell is a young man who's fallen down on his luck, but he's never been convicted of a crime, not even a traffic ticket," Kim Wan said. "He has been working with the probate court to establish his paternity and possible right to inherit, and has no intention of leaving without seeing that through. His plan is to return to the University of Texas as soon as his monetary situation allows."

"Plans are easily changed Your Honor," the prosecutor said.

"Bail is set at five hundred thousand dollars," Judge Crow said.

Davey's shoulders slumped.

"Your Honor, that is tantamount to no bail at all for my client. We are seeking a suitable shelter for Mr. Bell where he can live during the course of the trial," Kim Wan said.

"That's enough," Judge Crow said. "Find a secure place and I'll reconsider. For now, bail's set."

Davey looked around at Merit and held back tears.

After the bail hearing, Merit and Kim Wan interrogated Davey in the courthouse anteroom. It was a green painted square with metal furniture making it cold and uninviting.

"If there's something you want to tell us, now would be a good time," Merit said.

"Our defense depends on not contradicting our facts in any way. If we assert something, it must hold true," Kim Wan said.

"I was following Liam around, but I didn't kill him. I didn't even talk to him. I saw him sitting on the shoreline and went to find a warm spot for the night. I was on Lady Bird Lake asleep before sunup," Davey said.

"That's where the murder took place, Davey. You were on Lady Bird Lake and you told Detective Chaplain that," Merit said.

"Kim Wan, you told me to tell the truth, and besides, they already knew," Davey said.

"How did they know?" Merit said.

"Chaplain told me they had pictures of me watching Liam and that I was a creepy pervert. They said I murdered him," Davey said.

"That's when I told him to shut up," Kim Wan said to Merit.

15

Merit and Val met in the conference room of Merit's office, which also served as the law library. Legal tomes reached all the way to the ceiling on two walls. Known only to Merit and Betty, the bottom locked cabinets held the complete works of John Grisham, Scott Turow, Scott Pratt, and Michael Connelly's Mickey Haller legal thrillers. Most were signed and many were first editions. The third wall was solid glass looking over downtown Austin and the Colorado River.

The law books were mostly unnecessary, as everyone in the firm had access to LexisNexis online, but nothing replaced the smell and the feel of the books for Merit. Val handed Merit a folder of printed summaries from Lexis and pulled a few books with the full cases and placed them before Merit on the table.

"So," Val said. "How much time do we have to amend the petition and notify the court about Davey's paternity test?"

"Normally, you'd notify the court when you were made aware of any new information that would effect the estate. But, I think we can stretch it out for few weeks without appearing as if we're trying to hide something," Merit said.

"That looks right," Val said still reading from a book.

"Maybe we'll do all the amendments at once and just make that part of the update. Appear matter of fact about it," Merit said.

"If the judge doesn't like it, at least she can't assert there wasn't a practical angle to waiting for efficiency's sake."

"What if you piss off the judge and she stops allowing you to work with Kim Wan?" Val said.

"I don't think that's going to happen. My job is to defend the estate. If Davey is a legal heir, part of my job is to make sure he inherits," Merit said.

"Right," Val said.

"The question is whether Davey can inherit from Liam," Merit said. "We know he's the only heir unless Ag turns up some long lost relative. We know Davey was Liam's biological son who was not disowned. Our issue is whether Davey can inherit from Liam if he's convicted of murdering him," Merit said.

"I see," Val said.

"We don't have a slayer rule in Texas, so Davey can inherit anything except life insurance. That's covered under a different statute," Merit said.

"Liam didn't have any life insurance," Val said.

"Right, so does Davey get the estate?" Merit said, flipping through another section of the probate code.

"Here's something on conviction of a crime and inheritance," Val said.

"He hasn't been convicted, so unless he is, he should get the assets," Merit said.

"What if he's found guilty of killing Liam?" Val asked.

"We need to know the requirements around that issue. Pull Probate Code Section 41d," Merit said.

Val pulled the proper volume and flipped over to the correct page. Merit leaned in and they read it together.

"Convicted Persons and Suicides. No conviction shall work corruption of blood or forfeiture of estate, except in the case of a beneficiary in a life insurance policy."

"If Texas doesn't have a slayer rule, why doesn't Davey get the money anyway?" Val asked.

"Since we don't have a slayer rule, we use other legal concepts. In the old days, a concept named forfeiture through corruption of blood prevented criminals from inheriting. It's from old English law where anyone who committed a capital crime couldn't inherit," Merit said.

"Gotcha'," Val said.

"Texans didn't like that, probably because of all the unsavory characters that settled here," Merit said.

"There might not have been anyone left with a clean enough record to get anything after all the cowboys shot up the town," Val laughed.

"Something like that," Merit laughed too.

"So, Davey can inherit even if he's convicted?" Val asked.

"Not so fast, Kemosabe. We have another legal concept called constructive trust. It's a court-created remedy designed to prevent unjust enrichment due to malfeasance. It's an equity thing," Merit said. "It's the ain't right statute."

"There's no such thing," Val laughed.

"Well, it ain't right for someone to kill someone and benefit from it," Merit said.

Val made a note. Merit flipped through the rest of the volume but found nothing to add.

"Maybe we can get a little justice for Davey and for Liam," Merit said.

16

The next day, Ag set out on the one and one half hour drive from Austin to Llano. He drove past Marble Falls and the highland lakes that sparkled in the Texas Hill Country listening to a T-Bone Walker CD. He didn't need a map or GPS. To get to Llano he just got on Highway 71 and headed west into the beautiful rolling hills.

Ag got into town just in time for lunch and looked around for the cafe with the most cars out front to decide where to eat. Like most Texas small towns he'd travelled through, he had a choice of barbecue, Tex-Mex, homestyle cooking, or fast food. He settled on Coopers Old Time Pit Bar-B-Que because it had the longest line and he had been to the one in Austin with good result. He got behind a craggy faced man who looked like he knew how to sit a tractor. They chatted about the weather while they waited and Ag asked him if he'd ever heard of the Bell family.

"Yep, they used to live around here," the farmer said.

"Not anymore?" Ag asked.

"Don't think so, but if you come up empty handed, go over to the farm supply. They know everyone around here," the farmer said.

"Thanks," Ag said.

To order they had to pass by the pit to select their choice of meats. Ag selected the brisket and sausage before going inside for fixin's and sweet tea.

Ag ate at a long picnic table stocked with bread and jalapeño peppers under photos on the wall of Bob Wills, Pinetop Perkins and Billy Joe Shaver. While he waited for the Llano County Courthouse to re-open after lunch, Ag looked at the timeline that Val had prepared. He viewed Liam's whereabouts circa the year that Davey was born, then counted back to nine months before. There were several hill country music venues where Liam could have played around that time. The list included Longhorn Caverns State Park. Ag had been to several concerts there. Musicians and entertainers liked to perform at the caverns because the natural acoustics negated the need for microphones and amps.

Liam didn't seem like an unplugged type of musician, but you never know, Ag thought.

He continued through the list but there were only a couple of places that Liam could have performed during that time because it was the height of his career and he drew big numbers of fans around the area. The size of the venues would have limited his ability to use them. He saw on the list the dates that Liam had been nominated for album of the year and record of the year at the Grammy's.

How does one have it all and fall so far? Ag thought.

After lunch, Ag checked in with the Llano county clerk's office and proceeded to the bank of computers along the wall. The online records went back several years so Ag started at the computers to see if Louellen Bell was shown as owning any property. He pulled up the grantor and grantee records and ran her name in both.

"Nothing here," Ag mumbled.

He looked at his notes from the meeting with Davey and found Louellen's Mother's name, Sally Mae Bell. He ran Davey's grandmother's name through the same index with no luck there either.

To go back further through the records, he had to go to the old pre-computer deed books in the vault room. He went into the back and saw several landmen running standup oil and gas title at the long counter tops. He found a spot on a slanted table with an edge to hold the huge old books and opened the first pre-computer tome. He flipped to 'B' and checked the grantor page for Bell to see if either Sally Mae or Louellen had sold any property. No Bell, so he went to the grantee page under 'B' and checked to see if any Bell had purchased any property during the period covered by the book. He ran his finger down the long line of names. No luck.

He went back to the next prior year's book and looked only for Sally Mae as Louellen wasn't old enough to own property at that date. There it was. John Ray Bell and Sally Mae Bell purchased a home at 437 Elm Street in Llano, Llano County, Texas. Ag jotted down the volume and page and went to the clerk's desk to request a copy of the deed.

John Ray. Might be how Davey got his middle name, Ag thought. *Could still be from Liam, but maybe from his grandpa.*

Ag filled out the copy request and took it to one of the clerks behind the desk.

While Ag waited for the copy to be made, he checked his phone for email from Merit and found a note asking him to also check to see if Liam Nolan ever owned property in Llano County.

"That was my next step," Ag emailed in return.

He went through the same research routine again under 'N', checking the name Liam Raymond Nolan.

"There it is," Ag said aloud.

Several landmen who were doing research in the room looked up and chuckled. An aha moment wasn't unusual in property record rooms.

A deed from Liam Nolan to somebody for one hundred and thirty-five acres sold about the time that Liam started taking his nosedive into drugs.

Must have needed the money, Ag thought.

He went back to the clerk's desk and gave her another form with the volume and page of the deed to request a copy of it also.

His phone buzzed notice of an email in his in box. He opened it up since it was from Merit. It said: "P.S. If you have time would you pick up a case of wine from either Fall Creek Vineyards or Fly Gap Winery before you head back? Red. Pretty please!"

Ag smiled. "Of course I will."

Ag crossed to the other side of the clerk's office where the death and marriage license records were kept and conducted the appropriate search. He requested several documents at the front desk then found the men's room while the clerk filled his order. His mentor's number one rule had been never to pass a free bathroom when on the road. He remembered that every time he saw a sign with pants drawn on a stick.

After he picked up the docs, Ag went across the town square to Llano Honey Cafe and ordered a sweet tea.

He took a big gulp and reviewed the documents in his file and the new ones from the Llano County Clerk's Office.

He made a note in the file to go by the probate court and see if there was a record of who inherited the house from Louellen's parents. Might be siblings involved with Louellen.

Wonder why Davey was born in Austin and not in Llano? Ag thought.

Next, he ran through the marriage license of Louellen Bell. Married to George Pounder, dated after Davey's birthdate.

That explains why Davey doesn't claim him as his father, Ag thought.

♪

Ag proceeded to the Llano County Tax Assessor Collector's Office and asked for access to the current tax records. A quick look at the Elm Street property showed the taxes to be billed to Louellen Bell at the house address. The taxes appeared to be a year behind, and notice of overdue payment had been sent out three times.

The only logical means for Louellen to be the owner of record was through probate. He decided to skip the probate court records for now, as time was running short. He added a note to his list to follow up later if it seemed important.

Ag hit print screen and went over to the printer to obtain his copies. He paid for them at the desk, obtained a receipt, and filed the records in his folder.

Time for the town gossip, Ag thought.

17

Ag approached the double front doors of the Llano Farmers' Supply. Chicken coops and deer stands stood along one side of the building. The other side was lined with smokers, barbecue pits, and bales of hay. Upon entry, he smelled grain and saw twenty-five pound bags of deer corn stacked along the front wall.

Ag approached a pretty brunette clerk wearing a denim skirt and blue cowboy boots at the checkout line. Her name tag said *Valerie*. She smiled at Ag and he smiled back. He wanted to appear approachable to get answers to his questions.

"Hi, I'm over from Austin trying to find some old friends of the family," Ag said.

"Who ya' lookin' for?

"A family named Bell. John and Sally Mae Bell or their daughter Louellen," Ag said.

"I don't know them, but Miss Katie knows everybody that ever lived around here. She's behind that glass window over there. Just talk into the round hole on the front."

"Thanks," Ag said.

"Come back any time," she said.

Ag looked up at the window and sized up an elderly woman sitting behind it. She talked on the phone and appeared to be counting money out of sight below the glass line. He inspected a horse bridle and waited until she hung up. When she completed her call, he went over and said, "Howdy."

"May I help you?"

"I hope so. I understand you know everyone around these parts and I'm looking for the John and Sally Mae Bell family."

"I know 'em," Miss Katie said warily.

"I'm not a bill collector or anything like that," Ag said. "I just want to know what happened to the family. It's a probate matter. I know they still own a house on Elm,"

Ag saw Miss Katie relax a little.

"John and Sally Mae passed a long while back," Miss Katie said. "Their daughter Louellen inherited the house on Elm, but she doesn't hang around here much."

"Do you know where she lives?" Ag asked.

"Oh, she lives here all right. She just doesn't like it here," Miss Katie said with a look liked she'd sucked on a sour persimmon.

Ag waited. He hoped she wanted to say more. The best investigators knew when to ask a question and when to shut the hell up.

"She leaves to shack up with one guy after another in Austin or Waco or wherever, and comes back here when they kick her out or she gets tired of 'em," Miss Katie said.

"Sounds like a wild one," Ag prodded.

"You got that right. Let's just say she hasn't been to church since she was married. Her mother is probably turning over in her grave at that," Miss Katie said.

"What happened to Louellen's husband?" Ag asked.

"They didn't make it two years," Miss Katie said. "Fought all over town, yelling and screaming at each other."

"Did they have any children?"

"Not together. Louellen had one with some honky tonk musician. I think it was a son. Don't know what happened to the kid. The father left her and far as I know, never came back."

"Thanks, I owe you one," Ag said.

"Ain't nothin'," Miss Katie said.

Ag plugged the address of the Bell home on Elm Street into his GPS and drove across the railroad tracks, down a block, and into the driveway. He looked at the peeling paint, overgrown yard and sagging garage and surmised that no one cared much for the place. He peeked around the house into the back yard at an old rusty swing set and weedy garden plot.

He went back to the front door, saw no lights on in the window and knocked loudly, not expecting anyone to answer. He was right, nobody home. He went back to his truck, wrote a line requesting a call from the finder of the note and returned to the porch to wedge it into the front door.

He peeked into the mailbox and saw several ads and bills with Louellen's name on them but nothing to Liam Nolan or Davey Bell.

Another dead end, Ag thought. *At least I found the house.*

Ag made his last stop on the way out of town at the District Court building on Ford Street. He went into the District Clerk's office and asked to research the divorce records. He quickly found Louellen Bell Pounder and George Pounder's divorce decree.

Miss Katie was right. The date of the divorce was just over two years from the date on their marriage license. The decree of divorce showed no children of record and very little property to split. Louellen had not yet inherited the house on Elm, so no real property was listed. A few bucks in a bank account, clothing, and each had an older model car. Not much to show for a marriage. The occupations listed George as a drummer and Louellen as a back-up singer.

"A match made in heaven," Ag said.

Ag obtained a copy of the decree of divorce and checked his list while the clerk prepared the documents. The office closed when the clerk let him out and locked the door behind him.

He left town with a file full of paper that didn't amount to much, except the fact that Louellen was not married to George Pounder when she birthed Davey.

18

L.A. Baron sat in his office in Los Angeles. He listened to a music mix of Shakey Graves, Fat Tony and Gary Clark, Jr. while he worked. He'd flown back to attend a concert of one of his bands. Flintrocker was opening in the Hollywood Bowl. Of course, the band was a smash hit. Nothing L.A. attempted was done halfway.

L.A. opened the file on his desktop and made notes on a contract he'd had translated from Japanese to English. It granted TofuGrind the use of Liam Nolan's tune, *Fever Stomp*. TofuGrind, the Japanese film and video game company, had insisted on the choice of music. The song was one of the few that L.A. still had under contract from his time with Liam. He planned to take full credit and to suck every cent out of what was left in the management portfolio. Each new deal extended the contract expiration date and he intended to milk it as long as possible. If he could, he'd get his hands on the rest of Liam's portfolio too. That would be the comeback of the century.

"This could be a fun challenge," L.A. said, "I've never created a comeback for a dead man before. Might be the talk of the town."

Whereas L.A. couldn't carry a tune in a bucket or play any musical instrument with great skill, he had a sharp business mind and could smell a deal a mile away. He also had a knack for finding his opponents' weak spots and the timing to take advantage of it. What gave L.A. his biggest advantage was his ear. He could hear a band and know if they would make it immediately. He rarely missed when he took on a new group or stole an older group or performer from a rival manager. And he loved music. It was his soul and his heart. He just wished he didn't have to deal with musicians to get it.

"I made you Liam Nolan!" L.A. said to the album cover framed and mounted on the wall. "Time to collect."

He pushed the speaker button on his phone and summoned Ash Joyner.

"Come in quietly," L.A. said.

Ash entered with an iPad and sat at the Saarinen table that L.A. utilized for conferences. L.A. brought his laptop and joined him at the large white marble oval resting on a single pedestal.

"What's up?"

"I've gone through this contract with TofuGrind. They want Nolan's Fever Stomp. I've tried to sell them a song with the same tempo, style, mood and lyrical theme as Fever Stomp, but no go," L.A. said.

"That's too bad," Ash said.

"I'm not creating a comeback for Nolan without getting all of the goodies in his estate. What we have now is chicken feed," L.A. said.

"Who knew Liam Nolan would have a comeback," Ash said.

"Besides, the deal with TofuGrind is not set. I need to see how far I can push them on price. I'm considering royalties instead of a flat fee," L.A. said.

"Got it," Ash said.

"I want you to put together a meeting with legal. Keep it quiet. I'm ready to counteroffer on the Nolan contract. Let's get moving," L.A. said.

"Full legal staff?" Ash asked.

"No, only Cooper and Ward. No leaks. I don't want Billboard, Variety, or The Hollywood Reporter getting ahead of this deal. Last thing we need is that Texas lady lawyer or Nolan's bastard kid getting wind of my plans," L.A. said.

"I'm sure Merit Bridges has no idea. The estate is so small with what Nolan had left, no one would put forth much effort to get hold of it," Ash said.

"I'm counting on that. We'll get our money on *Fever Stomp*, but I don't want all his other records being played again without getting a piece of that action as well," L.A. said.

"Why not just get some income flowing in and show her you're the best guy for the job," Ash said.

"I'd be tipping my hand and she may hire one of my competitors," L.A. said. "Liam and I had already parted ways and were waiting for the contract to run out. Bridges is not likely to continue to work with me if those wishes were expressed to her."

"That's for sure," Ash said.

"By the time she finds out I've got a deal cooking for *Fever Stomp*, it will be too late."

"Why not sell TofuGrind something by Flintrocker or one of our other artists?" Ash said.

"As I said, I considered that. I pushed as hard as I could. They want this song. The video game developers wrote the game to the tempo of the song and the game's characters refer to several lines in the melody. Some guy in a garage who sold it to TofuGrind developed the whole thing stoned and listening to *Fever Stomp*," L.A. said.

"I understand," Ash said and shrunk back in his chair.

I understand you want it all, Ash thought.

"I'll try to buy the portfolio from the estate if I get a chance. We have to keep TofuGrind under wraps until the estate is settled. This will add millions to the probate. I want to have full control before Merit Bridges knows what hit her," L.A. said.

L.A. worked dark magic at his desk while Ash did his bidding in assembling the legal team. L.A. fired off emails, made phone calls and gave orders to minions all while sitting in the middle of his trophy wall of degrees, honorariums, platinum and gold records, and autographed photos with celebrities and politicians.

The music business had changed so much in the past few years that even L.A. had whiplash. The traditional music industry was built on the world of physical shelf space, vinyl and plastic. It was shepherded forward by MTV, AM/FM radio, and television. All that was in L.A.'s rear view mirror. It was replaced by digital downloads, on-demand streams and unlimited digital shelf space with inventory on demand.

The days of the major labels were over. Artists used TuneCore and CDbaby to deliver their music into iTunes, Spotify, Amazon, and the like. Aspiring artists had little to lose in getting their music out into the world. The need for L.A. had to be re-defined by the new rules, and he kept his eye on the ball even in his sleep. He had no intention of being passed up by all the new baby talent in L.A. He'd gotten where he was the hard way and planned to keep it all.

Later that day, L.A. slipped into the conference room which was already assembled to his specifications. Lawrence Cooper and Justin Ward, his primary legal advisors in Los Angeles, were present along with Ash. All were seated, allowing L.A. to be the tallest in the room until he sat, too. He spoke to the group like a madam with a whip.

"I want you to go over a contract in detail. It's on your mobile devices now. Make sure it's bullet proof and that payment can only come to me for distribution," L.A. said.

Cooper and Ward both looked at tablets before them and touched the screen to bring up the document marked *Nolan/TofuGrind Film & Video Agreement*.

"You can go through the fine print later. For now, my main concerns are keeping the income in light of Nolan's death, and not getting bogged down in the Texas probate while we are cutting this deal."

Cooper flipped the pages quickly to get an overview of the contract. Parties were shown as TofuGrind and Liam Nolan through its agent of record, Baron Entertainment Enterprises, with Nolan as copyright holder. Non-exclusive usage of *Fever Stomp*, credits on the film, film trailer, and video game, and advertising. Pages and pages followed.

"It will take some time to dissect all of the clauses," Ward said.

"Right. Also, read it in comparison to our old contract with Liam Nolan and make sure there are no loopholes between the two documents," L.A. said.

Cooper and Ward both nodded.

"My contract with Nolan extends as long as there's something in play that I have sold. Let's get this on the long payout plan," L.A. said.

"What about the video game music?" Ward asked.

"It's an issue. I know my contract with Liam doesn't cover it specifically, but I think we can make an argument that it extends to the video game through the film," L.A. said.

"I'll do some research on that issue," Ward said.

"Which is more important, the movie music or the music for the video game?" Cooper asked.

"There is no film without the video game so let's lead with that," L.A. said.

"Ok, I'll prioritize accordingly," Cooper said.

"Do you want a royalty on the video game or do you want a flat payment? Gambling or going for the sure thing?" Ward asked.

"I want a flat payment on the film to make some up-front cash. Second, I want a royalty on the video game in order to legally extend my contract with Liam. I don't know if this video game will go, but I'm willing to gamble on TofuGrind if they pay enough on the film rights," L.A. said.

"Got it," Ward said.

Cooper nodded and made notes.

"Is this an online game or a single use game?" Cooper asked.

"It's an online game. There's language in the contract which permits the transmission of the game over telephone lines, cable TV systems, cell phones, satellites and wireless broadcast," L.A. said.

"I'll add a clause to make sure it covers any future technology that may be developed that might utilize the song. As you know, online gaming can stretch far into the future if the game becomes popular," Cooper said.

"Right. Think World of Warcraft or League of Legends," L.A. said.

Cooper nodded and made more notes.

"Make sure the term of the contract is as long as the video game is in play," L.A. said.

"Worldwide territory for distribution?" Ward asked.

"Right," L.A. said.

"Will ASCAP track foreign performances and collect royalties for distribution back here in the states as usual?" Ward asked.

"Yeah, same as always," L.A. said. "Can't get around that."

"The Texas attorney may see it. That's public information. It can be monitored by anyone," Ward said.

"Yeah, but it's delayed and buried. It will take some work to dig it out. Hopefully, I'll have what I want before someone gets wise to the royalties," L.A. said.

After Cooper and Ward had written down their marching orders as given by L.A., they left for their respective offices to get to work on the contracts. Only L.A. and Ash remained.

"Call in HackerDude," L.A. said. "We need a distraction."

19

L.A. and HackerDude sat in L.A.'s office and peered into a laptop on the table before them. HackerDude wore an Edie Brickell t-shirt and jeans with holes in them. He looked the exact opposite of L.A. who had on a black Armani suit and oxblood Versace loafers – no socks.

HackerDude was an expert at gathering personal information without detection by monitoring websites, mapping sources, and financial data. He had already gotten Merit's social security number, driver's license, State Bar of Texas number, home address, her child's name and school address, her favorite charities, and a list of most of the men she had been with in recent years.

"Good, good." L.A. said. "Time to make the next move."

"What do you need?" HackerDude said.

"I want Bridges' mobile phone messages and texts to continue to go to my inbox on the proxy site. Let's set up a new proxy with a couple of layers of anonymity and start pulling in her office emails, too."

"She uses Tech Security out of Austin for encryption and email hosting. I could set up an alias in the back-end of the server that will distribute email to both Bridges and another address. It won't be easy. If I can't do that, I don't think I can pull the emails without being traced."

"What about hacking her password and reading her mail that way?" L.A. asked.

"They probably rotate passwords or use thumbprint login just like you do. Tech Security would recommend that. Whatever we do, they won't find us, but they may find out that information is going out. They might guess it's you," HackerDude said.

"They also might send bogus information to confuse us," L.A. said.

"Or, to catch us," HackerDude said.

"I don't want to risk that yet. I'll handle the bugging old school. For now, let's mine what we can safely get online," L.A. said.

HackerDude was providing internet vigilantism and hactivism for several political officials and other top executives. He was an expert at cyberstalking and had a reputation for cyberbullying as well. L.A. knew about a few of his clients, the ones who'd hooked them up. Most of them were hidden. L.A. liked that about HackerDude. Discretion was the number one job criterion for a black hat hacker. Nothing was personal to HackerDude. Strictly business.

"It's all about beating the technology," HackerDude said.

"No, it's all about beating the opponent. I want to set up some fake websites like the ones we did for Dog and Pony Band when they did their world tour. We'll need at least three, all news type sites," L.A. said. "I want to be able to post on the website, on Facebook, and on Twitter."

"You want more gossip or hard news?"

"Let's do one gossip type site like the Kardashian fans or People Magazine followers might read. Let's put up two that appear to be real news like *The Daily Beast* or *Huffington Post*. Let's also hit *The Austin Chronicle* when appropriate."

"How about a gossip story first to ease it into the public eye?" HackerDude said.

"That's good, and throw up a bunch of accurate news and backdate it so the sites look like they've been up for a while. Same for Facebook and Twitter. Make the history either gossip or hard news based on the site. Make it look credible."

"Of course. You want me to post the remaining fake news stories or do you want to?" HackerDude asked.

"You do the old stuff. I'll do the current posting. Just make it look real and get me the login info," L.A. said.

"On it," HackerDude said.

"Most importantly, make sure no one can trace it to me. Same as before," L.A. said. "I'll use the clues from emails on her law clerk Valentine Louis' computer to add some authenticity."

"Want me to post some real news each day to mix in with the fake news you'll be posting?" HackerDude asked.

"Good idea. Keep it going until I let you know to stop," L.A. said.

"You want algorithm tracking daily?" HackerDude said.

"Right. Let me know how we're doing with readers and if we need to make adjustments," L.A. said.

"Will do."

"Make sure the Austin public believes it," L.A. said.

"Of course they'll believe it. They've been told what to think and they will at least wonder. Why wouldn't they? Even smart, reasonable people get caught up in a good story," HackerDude said.

"Right."

"How about a fact check section on the websites? That way if people click through to the story and doubt it, they'll find some facts or quotes that will seal the deal." HackerDude said.

"Yes, good, "L.A. said.

"That will help with search engines as well," HackerDude said.

"Right," L.A. said.

"How about some fake documents too. Something on her letterhead or on the City of Austin letterhead?" HackerDude asked.

"Perfect," L.A. said.

"We can continue to monitor Valentine Louis. I'm tracking the info on his laptop, but unless he forwards email to his personal account or works from home, we might not get much. He works on a desktop at the office," HackerDude said.

"That was a gold mine with the info about the DNA results. Glad he sent the research memo on the probate to his home computer to work on it." L.A. said. "Keep trying on the office emails and go ahead and route the assistant's email through a new proxy site so I can see it in real time."

"Got it," HackerDude said. "I'll put in some notifications for key words so you don't have to read it all. What would you like to be tagged on?"

"Let's do Merit Bridges, probate, Liam Nolan, David Bell, and throw in my name too," L.A. said.

HackerDude clicked around on his laptop. "Done."

"Let's get some fake news going asap, and steal her thunder whenever we get the chance," L.A. said.

"Even when we put out the truth, we'll screw with her timing and throw her off guard if we can get the word out first," L.A. said.

"Timing is everything," HackerDude said.

"Right."

"Easy peasy," HackerDude said.

"I want to start doxing as much information as possible out of that law firm," L.A. said.

"Doxing? Pretty fancy word for online stalking. Have you been reading *Hacker Exposed* again?" HackerDude laughed.

"Just do it," L.A. said.

"Done," HackerDude said.

"And, I want to have a big story out by the end of the day tomorrow," L.A. said.

"Something newsworthy?" HackerDude asked and clicked up a few of Val's emails and Merit's old Facebook messages. Next, he checked the Austin Statesman for old newspaper clippings and Austin9Online TV for more recent stories.

"She's fond of young handsome men, it seems," L.A. said while looking at the screen.

"Just a bit of truth mixed in with the fake news is always best," HackerDude said.

"Adds a touch of credibility. Just what we need," L.A. said.

Back in his cave, HackerDude set to work. He had a scan-proof room in the basement of his house. The walls were covered with posters and wires hanging from hooks. He had a long table with multiple computers and laptops set up along the length of it. He sat in a two thousand dollar Aeron office chair that was adjustable to every joint in his body while he listened to an El Dusty live recording. This is where he worked his magic - black magic and cyberbullying.

He had dozens of screen names and had set up hundreds more for the benefit of his various clients. He could have a website up and running in a matter of minutes.

He used anonymous remailers that made it all but impossible for anyone to determine the true identity of the source of an e-mail. Then, he used various aliases for social media posts.

Anonymity emboldened HackerDude and his clients. It was the element that made their work effective, gave them an advantage, and allowed them to harass their victims without recourse from legal investigators. He was cold blooded and unstoppable.

20

Betty walked into Merit's office with a cup of tea and a big white box with a red bow on it. She put both on the desk and sat in one of the guest chairs.

"Looks like you have an admirer," Betty said.

"Hmmm," Merit said.

She ripped off the ribbon and opened the box. Inside were a pair of bright red boxing gloves and a note with Merit Lady Echo Bridges written in calligraphy on the envelope.

"Somebody did their homework," Merit said. "Not that many people know my full name."

"What is it?" Betty asked.

Merit pulled out the boxing gloves which were tied together with the laces. They spun and danced as she dangled them for Betty to see. Merit ripped open the envelope.

"You're a knockout! Thanks for your hard work," Merit read from the card. "It's from Texas KnockOut Illiteracy. A thank you gift."

"How nice," Betty said. "You deserve it."

"You helped," Merit said.

Merit walked over to the door and hung them on the coat hook.

"Maybe the gift will make this a little easier," Betty said.

"Oh no," Merit said.

Betty walked over and stood behind Merit looking at the computer. Betty hit a few keys on Merit's desktop over her shoulder and up popped a grainy picture of Merit with a younger man.

"Have you seen this?" Betty asked.

Merit scrolled down the online site called The Gossip According to Garpe. The top story of the day was a report about Merit having an affair with a twenty-five-year-old local actor named Billy Montgomery Wier. Purportedly, they had been caught on camera making out at an unnamed outdoor bar on Brazos Street.

"Oh, my God!" Merit said. "That's an old photograph taken at a science fair with Ace." The pic was photo-shopped giving Ace someone else's head that appeared twenty years older with the beginnings of a beard and wild hair.

"Google Alerts included it in my daily summary of news about you and the firm," Betty said.

"This is offensive. My own son," Merit said.

"Do you recognize the location or remember when you were wearing that outfit?" Betty asked.

"It sounds a lot like Cedar Door," Merit said. "The picture is definitely at Ace's science fair, but the photo is so shopped he's unrecognizable."

"Says it was taken at a bar," Betty said.

"That was at Ace's fifth grade school, not a bar," Merit said. "What is this site?"

"Never heard of it," Betty said.

Betty clicked around a few news stories and Merit took over the mouse and started clicking for herself.

"Looks like they only go back about two years," Merit said.

"They're quoting an unnamed source for the picture and the setting," Merit said.

They perused the site and saw a couple of gossip stories about Matthew McConaughey, Robert Earl Keen, and a few members of the City Council. Nothing was too damaging, just fodder for happy hour chat. The word *alleged* was used in most of the stories.

Merit clicked back to the story about her and the mysterious young man and read further.

"It says I've been seen around town hooking up with one of the members of Killer Elite but that my current unnamed boy toy is the flavor of the month," Merit said.

"Are you seeing anyone?" Betty asked.

"Not that I know of," Merit said.

"Says you couldn't be reached for comment," Betty said. "No one called this office from Garpe."

Merit saw the Facebook icon below the story and logged into her page to see if anyone had posted it. It wasn't showing on her page, but she had security blocks there. She searched her name and there it was all over social media with the grainy picture and comments by gossipers she didn't know.

"Get the IT nerds to see if they can find out who set it up," Merit said. "If they can't find the source, at least check the date the website was registered. At least we'll have a time frame."

"Some people have nothing better to do than this?" Betty asked.

"This is the way of the world now," Merit said.

"What are you going to do about it?" Betty asked.

"If I contact them, they can publicize what I write or say," Merit said. "Let's lie low and see if it blows over."

"Like a mobile home in a hurricane," Betty said.

Just down the street, L.A. sat in his Austin office reading a letter from The Law Office of Merit Bridges. It was a form letter addressed to 'Dear Sir or Madam', and gave some basic information to parties who may or may not have an interest in the estate of Liam Nolan.

"What a disrespectful bitch," L.A. said to the page. "She couldn't even individualize the letters for those of us who are obviously entitled to information. How rude!"

Minion Two appeared at the open door.

"Not now," L.A. said. "Close the door."

Minion Two did as he was told and disappeared behind the door.

"I'll teach Merit Bridges to tango with me," L.A. said as he threw open his laptop and clicked so hard the keyboard shook.

First, he went through this daily process of changing his password. It was not very convenient, and not considered a 'best practice' in the industry, but HackerDude had instilled in him the need for constant vigilance. Apparently, HackerDude had worked with a client in Los Angeles who had been lax about password protection and had led investigators to a kiddie porn site. According to the Dude, the oversight led to the indictment of over a dozen pedophiles and the conviction of ten of them. It may have been an exaggeration by HackerDude, but it stuck with L.A., and he took no chances. He made a mental note to see if HackerDude could set up three factor authentication instead.

L.A. clicked through to an area of his computer separated by a special firewall and opened a Scribd document-sharing account. He imported a copy of a news story from the *Austin Statesman* and began to edit it. He changed the name of the perpetrator to Merit Bridges and changed every third or fourth word so it could not be compared and identified easily.

The story showed a prior Dallas attorney, now Merit in Austin, as having a war room that her staff could only access with a special door code. The room was used to strategize secret actions on behalf of clients which were against the code of professional ethics of the State Bar of Texas and probably illegal. He included the names of a couple of Merit's big cases from the last two years and hinted that they may have benefited from this special war room and unethical strategies emerging from it. He heavily edited the rest of the story and when he was satisfied uploaded it to the site.

The news story appeared just like a clipping from the newspaper. It seemed authentic alongside all the other news stories and fake reports that HackerDude had included on the fake news sites.

L.A. created a link to the document and put the link into a fake tweet on one of his many faux Twitter accounts. He included just enough of the text to act as click bait through to the full story. He added an authentic photo of Merit standing on the courthouse steps that he'd found in a periodical. He retweeted the whole display several times through the other faux Twitter accounts. Other Twitter accounts began to pick it up, then it started trending with the hashtags #warroom #ethics.

He shared the link on Facebook and other social media sites until it got enough traction for people to go directly to the Scribd site. This enhanced the fake story's credibility because it didn't come from an unknown blog or possibly bogus website. Adding some famous, but fake, client's names was key to getting attention for the story. Anyone who didn't know Merit would probably know one of the fake client's names.

It went viral!

♪

Merit called Red Thallon and left a message.

Red called back right away and she and Merit discussed the fake news story about the war room.

"Want to give me a quote?" Red asked.

"No. I want you to tell me how to counter this. What purpose does it serve to slander me with something like this and how do I get rid of it?" Merit asked.

"I'll check around. Once it's out there, it's there. Best thing to do is not give it too much attention. Who are your enemies?" Red asked.

"I didn't know I had any outside of the legal realm. We usually fight it out in court and other legal ways," Merit said.

"Well, somebody is either up to mischief or serious business," Red said.

"Monkey business," Merit said.

"I'll run something if you'd like. But, if it's not true, I'd advise against it," Red said. "The more readers that talk about it, the more real it becomes."

"You'd think people would figure it out," Merit said.

"Just the opposite, the more times readers see it, the more likely they are to believe it. There's a professor at Vanderbilt who's working with Google's brainchild CrossCheck to debunk false information. It's for just this scenario. For now, you're stuck battling a dark web ghost without many weapons," Red said.

21

L.A. logged on to his special account that was recording everything in and out of Valentine Louis' laptop computer at his apartment in Austin. L.A. had not been able to access Merit's computers at work, but he was able to get to anything taken off premises. Val was apparently a clothes horse with a browsing history including Flashback, Blue Velvet, and Haute. He was popular too with thousands of Facebook friends and daily emails with buddies. The work emails were mixed in with the personal ones.

L.A. scanned the subject line of dozens of emails until he came across one entitled *Liam's Sponsor*. L.A. opened it and read through the entire thread. He surmised that a man named Reverend Morton Hightower had been part of Nolan's support system, he ran a shelter in East Austin, and he was expecting money for his charity from Liam Nolan's estate. According to the email, it had been part of the testamentary plan Liam had set up.

L.A. logged out and hit the button on his office intercom.

"Come," L.A. said into the speaker.

Ash entered the office and stood at the door waiting to be invited to sit, speak, or roll over.

"Do you still have those disguises we used to go to the Dog and Pony Band concert at the Hollywood Bowl?" L.A. said.

"You want to do another show and not be recognized?" Ash asked.

"No, something more covert."

♪

L.A., with Ash driving, circled the block a couple of laps to get a look at the St. John's Thrift Shop and Men's Shelter in East Austin. They parked the big black Escalade on a back street a few blocks down and looked around. It was early evening, and no one of interest was out on the residential street. They exited the vehicle and walked toward St. John's. The neighborhood was clearly another example of gentrification. They turned the corner and entered an area of mixed residential and commercial properties.

"They must own this land to still be in this area of town. That or someone is renting cheap to cover the taxes while prices rise," L.A. said.

"Yeah. There's Rainey Street right across the freeway," Ash said as he looked up at the skyline full of cranes and high rises towering between them and downtown Austin.

They were dressed for the occasion in army jackets, tan Dickies work pants, and scuffed work boots. L.A.'s underwear and socks cost more than his entire outer garb. A day's growth of beard and George Strait gimme caps hid their faces. Hanging out with the less advantaged was something L.A. had been running from his entire life. He'd clawed his way out of St. Louis with a guitar pick and didn't plan to ever return. He sent money, and no one back home complained. For now, he'd play the part of the down-and-out to get what he wanted. They paused outside the door of St. John's.

"We want to find out about their operation and casually meet a guy named Reverend Hightower if possible. Don't be conspicuous," L.A. said.

"Am I wanting to live here, donate, or recover?" Ash asked and laughed.

"I think we want to volunteer or get services. Be helpful. But, act as if we don't have much money, so volunteering would be good," L.A. said.

"Got it," Ash said.

"Snap some pics with your phone if you can do it without being observed," L.A. said.

"Will do," Ash said.

"There's a bit of a crowd inside. Looks like dinner time," L.A. said.

L.A. and Ash entered St. John's dining hall and looked around for Reverend Hightower. The room was large and open. One end resembled an old hospital waiting room. The other end was piled high with boxes of donated clothing and small appliances. In the middle, dozens of men sat on benches at long picnic style tables. L.A. spotted a bearded man in a black robe that looked like a duster from an old western. He was leaning over a table serving cornbread and rolls from a basket and spreading good will and smiles to the various diners.

Ash stopped a man who was walking toward the serving line.

"Is that Reverend Hightower?" Ash asked and gestured toward the black robed server.

"Yeah, that's him," the homeless man said without making eye contact.

Ash surreptitiously snapped a picture of Hightower.

L.A. waited for Reverend Hightower to empty his basket and followed him toward the kitchen.

"Hello. I was told you are in charge here," L.A. said as he extended his hand.

Ash hung back and watched.

"That's right. I'm Reverend Hightower," he said and shook hands with L.A.

"I wanted to stop by and meet you because my friend here is in recovery and needs a place to plug in for support while in Austin," L.A. said.

"You two new in town?" Reverend Hightower asked Ash.

"Yeah, he just got in from L.A.," L.A. said.

"What's your drug of choice?" Reverend Hightower asked.

"Booze mostly," Ash said.

L.A. watched the reverend observe Ash. Hightower had a quizzical look on his face.

"All are welcome here," Hightower said. "You hungry?"

"No, I just fed him," L.A. said.

"You need a place to stay?" Hightower asked.

"No, just some support for the booze and a place to hang out where I won't get into trouble," Ash said.

L.A. gave Ash a hard look.

Hightower walked over to a table of pamphlets and business cards and selected a few brochures.

"Here's some basic information on our hours and rules. Come back tomorrow and we'll get you into a group. There are a couple of forms to fill out, but what we require most is a willingness to show up on a regular basis and participate."

Ash took the paperwork. L.A. extended his hand to Hightower.

"I appreciate the help for my friend," L.A. said.

"See you around," Hightower said as he shook hands with both men.

"Right," L.A. said.

"Who are you and what are you up to?" Hightower said to himself as they exited the shelter.

L.A. and Ash returned to the Escalade and once locked inside started laughing.

"That was too easy," Ash said.

"Don't be so sure. Hightower has seen a lot of liars. He may not know what we're lying about, but he knows we're not on the up and up," L.A. said.

"You think?" Ash asked.

"I do," L.A. said.

"Hmm," Ash said.

"It's okay. It tells me something that he was willing to play along," L.A. said.

"Right," Ash said.

"You sure jumped in quickly when he asked if you needed a place to stay," L.A. said.

"Who, me?" Ash said.

"Yes, you," L.A. said.

"I'll hang around and spy for you, but I'm not living in that slum," Ash said.

"All right for now. We can always move you in later if it becomes expedient to do so," L.A. said.

Ash looked out the window and did not smile.

22

L.A. returned to his Austin office and told Ash to go home for the night. He played a mix from his computer of Leon Bridges, Wade Bowen and Charley Crockett on his external speakers. Next, he logged into one of the many websites that HackerDude had set up and posted some small gossip stories about Merit and her continuing dalliances with younger men. Next, he went to the fake hard news sites and put up a couple of stories about her, including clients he'd gleaned from Val's laptop. Just enough to get things rolling.

L.A. poured himself a glass of Genius South Austin small batch gin from the bar. He inhaled the juniper and lime and took a long pull. He returned to his desk and dreamed about winning. He would win the entire estate. Once he set a goal, he always got all he wanted. He could see his bank balance rising in his mind's eye. He could not lose.

The gin warmed him inside and he began to reminisce. He tried to push away the thoughts, but they came on more strongly with each resistance. He couldn't stop the memory. His brother, his fraternal twin, pushing his face into the dirt. Calling him shrimp, shorty, tiny. He had worshiped his brother when he was a toddler, but by the time they were teenagers, Dahl, born two minutes before L.A., was twice his height and three times his heft. Dahl could play any musical instrument without much practice, and he had perfect pitch when he sang. His garage band was starting to get attention all over the Midwest, but it all ended. Dahl was dead and buried in St. Louis. L.A. could not bear to think about Dahl and what he had done to him. He couldn't bear it and he couldn't stop it.

L.A. finished his drink and started to pour another. Instead, he put down the glass and went to the closet.

He bolted the door and sat on the hard stool. He thought of Dahl with regret. He could not get the image of his brother from his mind.

He rocked to the words in his head. "I'm so sorry. I didn't mean it. I'm so sorry." The words became a mantra.

It did not comfort him. He rocked himself harder from side to side on the stool until a gurgle began in his throat and worked its way up to his mouth. It erupted in a growl that turned into a wail that shook his entire body and caused him to raise his feet from the floor. He trembled and shuddered until he slumped like a rag doll and his head lolled from side to side.

After the release, he sat for a long time as calm returned and he realized there were tears on his cheeks. He wiped them away with the back of his hand and sucked in the snot from his nose.

He became rigid and mumbled about Dahl, Merit, Liam, past enemies, and his authority over them. His life's work. His triumph over Dahl and all others who would stop him. He grumbled and cursed until he stopped rocking and pumped himself up into his full stature. He clenched his fists and stood up. He set his jaw, opened the door, and went back to his desk. He downed the last of the gin and went out into the dark night.

23

Ag and Chaplain had a meeting in Chaplain's office to discuss Merit's dilemma.

"This cyberstalking of Merit Bridges has gotten out of hand. There's another news story almost every day, and somehow the online stalkers are connecting the dots to naming Merit's clients. Just today, there was a new story about how she had unethically won a case and another about her overbilling her clients. Is there nothing else APD can do?" Ag asked.

"We've had some recent training on these types of issues since they're becoming more prominent," Chaplain said. "The cases are very hard to solve and even harder to prosecute."

"Even if you know who's doing it?" Ag asked.

"It's like trying to grab a water balloon. You squeeze it on one end and the liquid moves to the other end," Chaplain said.

"She's being harassed and embarrassed in the public eye," Ag said.

"Cyberstalking cases differ from regular stalking in that it's all technologically based, but most cyberstalkers escalate their harassment to include physical stalking as well. Forewarned is forearmed," Chaplain said.

"I'll add some extra security around her," Ag said. "We still don't have a handle on who's doing it."

"A cyberstalker uses threats, fear, and intimidation to harass the victim. They can go so far as to exert financial control or even ruin a victim's credit," Chaplain said.

"I'll advise her to put some extra security in place around her finances," Ag said.

"Usually, the stalker tries to isolate the victim by harassing family and friends. Maybe a client. Everyone around her should be on guard," Chaplain said.

"When does it become a crime?" Ag asked.

"It's probably already a criminal act and I'm glad you're keeping us up to date. In deciding whether a situation is truly stalking, the victim should consider whether the perpetrator is acting with malice and premeditation. Stalking activities are often obsession-based vendettas," Chaplain said. "Does anyone fit that description?"

"Not that we've identified so far," Ag said.

"Have Merit go through her client files and make a list of any likely suspects. We'll do what we can to check them out, but until the perp reveals him or herself, we'll be guessing," Chaplain said as he turned and pulled a three-ring binder from a shelf.

"She's picky about revealing client information. That may be easier said than done. What's that?" Ag said.

"It's the info from the workshop on cyberstalking. I think the situation with Merit may be called cyberbullying," Chaplain said.

"What's the difference?" Ag asked.

"Says here cyberbullying is the use of information technology to repeatedly harm or harass in a deliberate manner. According to U.S. Legal definitions, cyberbullying could be limited to posting rumors or gossip about a person on the internet, bringing about hatred in other's minds, or it may go to the extent of personally identifying victims and publishing materials severely demeaning and humiliating to them."

"That's definitely the case here, and it's getting worse," Ag said.

Chaplain flipped to a tab in the back of the notebook.

"There's a case study here from 2003. Appears a woman contacted police claiming someone had given her private info, including her location and description, to men through a dating service. The woman discovered the act when she was contacted by two different men. Each man said that they had previously talked with her and arranged a personal encounter. The post included private info including a semi-nude photo, her phone number and home address," Chaplain said.

"What else does that book say? Any way to stop it?" Ag asked.

Chaplain flipped through a few more pages.

"Not without knowing who the perp might be. Key factors include false accusations. A cyber-stalker often tries to damage the reputation of his victim by posting false information on social media websites or blogs. A perp may even create fictitious websites or accounts for the purpose of spreading false rumors and allegations about the victim. Stalkers may hire an investigator to gather data and interact with colleagues, monitor victim's activities, and even encourage others to harass the victim."

"That's a lot of work. To what end?" Ag asked.

"Control. It's all about control," Chaplain said.

"And, that's usually linked to a big ego or a need for revenge or both. Either way, that leads to instability and it's dangerous," Ag said.

"It is dangerous, and don't forget old fashioned greed on your list of motives," Chaplain said.

Merit, Ag and Steve Parson, the IT nerd from Tech Security, sat in the conference room of Merit's office.

"There have been three more stories and two more pictures posted on various social media sites since we called you. Someone is coming at us with all this technological propaganda and it's hard to tell where they're going. I need to make sure my clients' information is secure," Merit said.

"Somehow, they are getting names from our client list, even those that are not publicly known to be associated with the firm," Betty said.

"I've re-checked all the office computers and they are secure. The phones should be fine, Apple has just updated security around that, Parson said.

"That's a relief," Betty said.

"As far as the fake news sites, I've searched the wayback machine to see if the site has been cached. So far, no luck there. I've checked the website domain and it's recent. That's no surprise," Parson said.

"Can you tell who registered it?" Betty asked.

"Yes, it's registered to an alias for someone who's really good at this." Parson said.

"If you can give me the dates that the sites were set up, maybe I can limit my suspect list for the police to the dates near those. As you can imagine, I'm reluctant to give them a full list," Merit said.

"I'll keep prying into it. Please send me anything new that appears about you or the firm, and let me know if you have reason to believe there's been a breach of your office records," Parson said.

"Let's stop this before that happens," Merit said.

"That's what we're here for," Parson said.

"Well, it's not working," Ag said.

Betty shook her head.

24

L.A. and HackerDude met at L.A.'s office in Los Angeles on a Saturday morning. L.A. had been flying out of Austin as often as possible. He much preferred the L.A. club scene with the beautiful people to that of Austin with the old hippies, students, and new hipsters mixed in. Of course, HackerDude was never invited for a Los Angeles night out or to Austin. He wasn't beautiful enough, and L.A. needed to keep his distance from hackers.

"I need to cultivate more from her phone," L.A. said. "I'm not getting everything I need from her office."

"I'm working on it. You've got her location at all times. Anything more and she might detect it," HackerDude said.

"What if we route it to a burner phone and I monitor it from there?" L.A. asked.

"That's a given, but what's out there in terms of hacking software is risky," HackerDude said.

"We still have the old-fashioned bug. It's only good for her office, but it's better than nothing," L.A. said. "I want more."

"There's some new malware, code named Pegasus 2. It hacks into a victim's iPhone in a single click. It's been dubbed a "one tap" attack because the iPhone user only has to click on one link for it to become effective," HackerDude said.

"Never heard of it," L.A. said.

"It was discovered when this human rights lawyer in the United Arab Emirates became suspicious when he received a text which promised to expose secrets about people undergoing torture in the Islamic State," HackerDude said.

"What does it give me that I don't already have?" L.A. asked.

"It will turn her phone into a digital spy in her purse. It's capable of employing the iPhone's camera and microphone to snoop on activity in the vicinity, record messages, and login to chat apps. It basically backdoors every communications mechanism on the phone. It steals all the information in the Gmail app, all the Facebook messages, contacts, Skype, WeChat, Telegram, you name it."

"Amazing," L.A. said. "I want to track her so I can post the photo-shopped pictures of places she actually frequents."

"A touch of truth to add to the credibility," HackerDude said.

"Right," L.A. said.

"Pegasus will do the trick. It's the most sophisticated virus of its kind, the equivalent to a remote jailbreak," HackerDude said. "Only one thing."

"What's the problem?" L.A. asked.

"Downside is that Apple has discovered the predecessor, Pegasus 1, and they've updated all of the security against it. Someone in a law firm would have added security to cover that. Apple is watching now, and they'll discover Pegasus 2 quickly," HackerDude said. "Even if it does work for a while, since this is considered weaponized spyware designed by that Israeli cyber arms dealer, the consequences for getting caught are very severe."

"Haven't they built in something to avoid detection?" L.A. Asked.

"Sure, breaking down the program has been compared to defusing a bomb. It has a hair-trigger self-destruct, so no problem there. But, if I knew what I was looking for, I could detect it, and that means others can as well. You'd be gambling that she wouldn't hire the right expert to catch it before it blew up," HackerDude said.

"What if she did?" L.A. said.

"She might not be able to trace it all the way to you, but eventually someone may put two and two together and your name will come up," HackerDude said.

"Let me worry about that. How long can we get away with it before we'd have to shut down Pegasus 2?" L.A. asked.

"No way to know," HackerDude said. "Maybe a few weeks, maybe a few months. It will take me some time. It will cost you."

"Let's run it," L.A. said.

"Didn't you go to the Blackhat Hacker's Conference in Vegas? Some genius there should know how to get around this phone security."

"That's how I found out about Pegasus. At the last Blackhat, there were more hackers than law enforcement in Vegas. We need to keep an eye on what the good guys are doing to stay one step ahead. This stuff wasn't even online yet."

"I thought you tried not to be seen in public," L.A. said.

"Sometimes it's better to listen over drinks to what people are saying. That only happens in person. You're not the only one with disguises," HackerDude said.

"How do you know about that?" L.A. said.

"Oh, just a guess. Most famous people have a way to skulk around when they need to. Besides, it's worth the risk for the info," HackerDude said.

"Right," L.A. said.

"And I have a new trick for you that you're going to love," HackerDude said.

L.A. went to favorites on his internet browser and opened Billboard Magazine online. He clicked through the appropriate links to Japan's top One Hundred Songs of the week and scrolled down past Bruno Mars, Koi, and Monochro. He kept scrolling until he hit number eighty-eight, and there it was, *Fever Stomp* by Liam Nolan.

While he was elated, he didn't know how much longer he could keep it under wraps in the United States. Nolan's comeback was knocking at the proverbial door.

"What's my next move?" L.A. asked himself as he drummed his fingers on his desk.

He clicked up his calendar and calculated eighteen months until the online game would hit the U.S. Twenty-four months until the film would be released. He backed up six months for both and took a guess that someone who was not in the music business would not realize what was happening until then. So, he had roughly two months to get control of the estate from Merit.

"Let's see how I can screw her over today," L.A. said.

25

L.A. flew into terminal one at Nashville International Airport on his private Lear jet 75 known for its efficiency and quiet ride. The airport call sign BNA stood for Berry Field Nashville, but only the military facilities at the airport still used the name. Nashville, the Songwriting Capital of the World reminded L.A. of Austin, the Live Music Capital of the World. *Each city is claiming a spot in the name game*, L.A. thought.

"This won't take long," L.A. said to the pilot upon exiting the plane. "Keep the engine running."

The pilot laughed.

L.A. went down the jetway and sat at the quietest table he could find at Tootsie's Orchid Lounge. It was a hopping spin-off of the historic Nashville honkey-tonk that L.A. had frequented many times on his trips to Music City. A small combo played cover music in the opposite corner. The lead singer animated his body while riffing on a Maren Morris tune as if he were playing to a crowd of thousands.

"Everyone wants to be a rock star," L.A. said.

"Pardon me?" the waitress said.

"Oh, just talking to myself. I'll have a Hendrick's Gin with a touch of tonic and lime."

"Coming right up," the waitress said and moved toward the bar.

A slight woman, even more petite than L.A., wound her way through the tables and chairs and sat across from him. She looked like she'd been rode hard and put up wet. Her hair was almost straw from over-processing, and the heavy makeup she wore had settled into the creases in her face and neck.

"I'm Louellen Bell," she said.

"Figured as much. Drink?" L.A. said.

"I'll have what you're having," Louellen said.

L.A. held up two fingers to the waitress who was holding a tray full of empty glasses and dishes. She nodded in acknowledgement.

"Glad you could make it," L.A. said.

"I'm always interested in anything new," Louellen said.

A male muscular type with a sleeve of colorful tattoos on his right arm stood by the bar and watched the two converse.

"Your bodyguard?" L.A. asked.

"Something like that," Louellen said. "I saw you in Austin at Liam's funeral."

"Was that him driving the car?" L.A. asked.

"Yep," Louellen said and bit on an unfiltered cigarette.

"Didn't know they made those anymore," L.A. said. "You can't smoke in here."

"I know, just getting ready. It's better for you than the ones with filters," Louellen said.

"Different cancer, same result," L.A. said.

Louellen chewed on the tobacco stick and out of habit pretended to blow the smoke over her right shoulder through the side of her mouth.

"You flew all the way here. Want to tell me what you want and why we couldn't talk about it on the phone?" Louellen asked.

"Obviously, it's about Liam and his son Davey," L.A. said.

"I don't know who Davey's father is. Maybe it's Liam, maybe it ain't," Louellen said.

L.A. could tag a liar and a bad negotiator from a mile away.

"That ship has sailed. DNA doesn't lie," L.A. said.

"So, what's it to you?" Louellen said.

"I have a small interest in Liam's portfolio. I thought you might have a small interest yourself," L.A. said.

"A small interest that pays for flying from Austin and taking your time to come here in that million-dollar suit?" Louellen said.

"I've never owned a suit that cost a million," L.A. said.

"You know what I mean," Louellen said.

L.A. acted cool by pretending to text and avoiding eye contact. He Googled Ryman Auditorium. He seemed to recall that Cody Johnson or Cody Jinks were on stage later.

"Let's just say I want to position myself to manage Liam's estate. I think you have a legitimate claim to some of the funds, and if we work together, we may both be able to get ahead," L.A. said.

"A little something for retirement?" Louellen asked.

"Maybe," L.A. said.

"What do you have in mind?" Louellen asked.

"I think the State Bar of Texas should be a nice place for you to file a complaint," L.A. said.

"Why can't I file in court to get the estate?" Louellen asked.

"Do you have a claim against the estate?" L.A. asked.

"Maybe," Louellen said.

"We don't want you committing perjury on the record now, do we?" L.A. laughed.

26

The next day, Merit opened her Facebook page to find friend requests from a dozen men of various ages. All their pages had few photos and all were of themselves in various forms of erotic dress or undress. She refused them all.

She scrolled down her personal page and found a photo-shopped picture of herself dancing on a bar in what looked like a Coyote Ugly outfit. In the photo, she had on chaps, a bikini top, and cowboy boots with spurs. She expanded the picture on her screen and looked around the edges. The original photo was taken in The Texas Rose, owned by her client Slag. She hadn't seen him in months, as his legal work was sporadic. And she'd never danced there. She took a screen shot of the picture, deleted it from her page, and picked up the phone.

"Slag, this is Merit Bridges."

"Long time. How are you, Darlin'?" Slag said.

Merit could hear a Beyonce' tune playing in the background.

"Not so great. I have a stalker who's messing with me. I just found a photo-shopped picture I'd like to show you," Merit said.

"Sounds like more than a joke," Slag said.

"How many people know that I'm your attorney?" Merit asked. "I'm trying to find any clue to pinpoint who's doing this."

"Everyone. I don't keep it a secret," Slag said. "What can I do to help you?"

I'd like to run by and see you this afternoon if you're not too busy," Merit said.

"Never too busy for you Darlin'. Come on by anytime. I'll be here all day," Slag said.

She clicked over to the law office Facebook page, found it clear of issues, sent the screenshot of the bar dancer to Ag with a note about going to meet with Slag, and logged off.

"You better not enjoy this, Ag," she said to the email.

Merit entered the Texas Rose in East Austin beneath a large yellow blossom painted on a sign over the door. Merit reminded the bikini clad hostess that she was Slag's attorney. As usual, the main club and dance floor were closed off behind double doors to the right.

"He's expecting me," Merit said.

The hostess climbed the stairs up to the office. Merit watched her execute the climb in four-inch heels as she had seen other receptionists do, but this hostess had yellow roses tattooed on her calves and a vine winding up her thigh and into her bikini bottom.

That's a new one, Merit thought.

Slag came down quickly and escorted Merit into the interior of the club. It was bathed in colorful neon light. The pool tables were busy, even though it wasn't yet five o'clock. A dancer was twirling around one of the floor-to-ceiling metal poles on the stepped-up stage as a spotlight highlighted her sexy figure sans top.

"Sit here, Darlin'," Slag said and pulled out a stool at the back bar.

A stocky bartender doing double duty as bouncer came over.

"What'll you have?"

"Dublin Dr. Pepper," Merit said.

"Water," Slag said.

ZZ Top's *Legs* started to play and a new dancer attacked the pole. The pool players admired the show for a moment then went back to their game.

After they'd sipped their beverages for a few minutes, Merit opened her iPad and showed Slag the photo-shopped picture she'd snagged off her website.

"This is definitely your club. Any idea who took it?" Merit asked.

"Looks like an old photo of Brandy during rodeo season last year. We did a week with a cowboy theme. Anyone could have taken it, but it looks like a shot from our website. The background is behind the front bar. See," Slag said and pointed to the edges of the photo.

"Yep, I thought I recognized that neon sign," Merit said.

"Someone probably got it off the site and put your head on it," Slag said. "May I?"

"Sure" Merit said.

Slag took the iPad and entered TexasRose.com in the browser. Up popped the website for the club. He clicked through what seemed like a million pictures and came to a set of snapshots with a cowboy theme. Dancers were attired in everything from hats and boots to chaps and fringe.

"Here it is," Slag said after he'd located the shot of Brandy on the bar.

"Yep, that's it," Merit said. "I was hoping it was an original photo that I might trace through your surveillance cameras. No such luck."

"Sorry, Darlin'," Slag said. "You'll have to catch this critter another way."

27

Another round of fake news hit the internet the next day. Ag and Merit had scheduled a meeting to go over Liam Nolan's probate research so Ag was already in Merit's office.

"I don't know why this boy toy information keeps surfacing about me," Merit said.

"Well, it might be because you have a reputation for seeing men who are younger than you are," Ag said.

Merit scowled at him.

"Any trace on that photo from the Rose?" Merit asked.

"No. Dead end," Ag said.

"Says here I'm paying for sex by keeping these boy toys on my law office payroll," Merit said. "Says Val is one of my conquests. It just gets worse and worse."

"Where there's smoke there's usually fire," Ag said.

"You know Val is gay and you also know exactly who's on my payroll," Merit said.

"Yes, but there is a history there with younger men," Ag said.

"So, what? That's no one's business but my own," Merit said.

"Are you seeing the young guy in the Cedar Door picture?" Ag asked.

"How can you ask that? That is Ace with someone's head photo-shopped in. Why don't you believe in my ability to make my own choices?" Merit asked.

"Of course, I believe in you, Merit. Just tell me it's not true." Ag said.

"I just did. Besides, I don't owe you an explanation, Ag," Merit said.

Ag looked away.

"In fact, this subject is off limits. Let's keep it professional," Merit said. "I've got enough people on my back without having you there too."

"Sure, Merit, sure," Ag said.

Betty walked in with a stack of files and put them on Merit's desk.

"I need to go to El Paso for a couple of days on another case," Ag said. "I'll get everything to Chaplain before I leave town."

"Fine," Merit said.

"Fine," Ag said.

"Is this the right time to leave Austin?" Betty asked.

Both Merit and Ag stared at her.

"Guess so," Betty said as Ag stormed out the door.

Betty sat down in the guest chair.

"I can't believe Ag would question whether these things were true," Merit said.

"He doesn't doubt you, Merit," Betty said.

"Well, it sure sounds like it," Merit said.

"He just doesn't want to let go of his dream and face reality," Betty said.

"What reality?" Merit asked.

"That you are not his," Betty said.

132

28

Betty showed Gilbert Johnson into Merit's office. He had on a pair of jeans with a threadbare short-sleeved shirt and worn skinny tie. He wore newish shoes sans holes with one brown and one black sock. His lanky hair was slicked back as if he'd recently washed it.

"You look nice, Gilbert," Merit said and shook his hand.

"I went to St. John's shelter by my house. They have a room of donated clothes and showers. I dressed up for meeting with my lawyer," Gilbert said.

"That would be me," Merit smiled.

Gilbert blushed.

"I'm impressed, and I have good news. Take a seat," Merit said.

Gilbert sat in one of the guest chairs in front of Merit's desk and hugged his tattered file to his chest.

"I've ordered your title work. The title company will give us a preliminary title report that we can then use later to get title insurance for your buyer. That's how this goes. You must make sure the title is good – that you own it. I'll let you know when the report comes back," Merit said.

"How do I pay for that?" Gilbert asked.

"It's paid at closing," Merit said.

"Okay," Gilbert said.

"I spoke with the architect. He is still interested in purchasing your property and is willing to work with us on timing. We could give him first option to purchase," Merit said.

"That is good news," Gilbert said.

"It would be good to be able to tell the city that you have a possible buyer. It will help with time for getting the taxes cleared up. If we don't like his offer, you don't have to accept it," Merit said.

"So, we wouldn't sell it to him," Gilbert said.

"You might, but he has to pay market value. The only way to know for sure what the market is would be to put the house up for sale and see what kind of interest you get. Or, we could have an appraisal done. That's iffy on your property because it's one of the few tracts left in east Austin, and that makes it more valuable," Merit said.

"So, would someone build a new home?" Gilbert asked.

"Probably not. The buyer will probably go to the city and re-zone the site for commercial use. It's more valuable as a store or restaurant than a house. The contract will probably be contingent on the change in zoning, but it should be a cinch since most of the property around yours is commercial," Merit said.

"I understand. If it's a restaurant, maybe I'll eat there some day," Gilbert said.

"You might. There's another thing. Part of our training with Austin Legal Advantage is to help our clients not only get their money when we can, but help them with a plan to keep it," Merit said.

"A plan?" Gilbert said.

"I know you're a smart man, but it's a jungle out there, and I want to assist you with setting up whatever needs you have for using the funds once you receive them," Merit said.

"I hadn't gotten to the part about having the money yet," Gilbert said.

"Today may not be the day for you to create a plan, but soon there'll be a need for it and we should be ready," Merit said.

"Like what?" Gilbert asked.

"Well, you could set up a special account at an investment firm or credit union so that they only give you a certain amount per month, like an allowance. That way, you can live a long time on the money. Or, you could set up a co-signer on a regular bank account so no one can steal from you. If you ever withdraw over fifty dollars or so, it takes two signatures. No one could make you sign a check, or if you ever lost one or someone forged one, you'd be covered."

"I never thought of that," Gilbert said.

"There are lots of plans depending on what you want and how you see yourself living," Merit said. "How about you look at this brochure from Austin Legal Advantage, give it some thought, and we'll talk about it again before the closing."

Gilbert opened the colorful brochure, refolded it, and put it in his shirt pocket. He patted it through his shirt.

"No one's going to get my money," Gilbert said.

"That's right," Merit said.

As Merit walked Gilbert to the reception area, she noticed a woman wearing about twenty pounds of diamonds and a suit that cost more than the chair she was sitting in. Merit looked at the receptionist with a question mark on her face.

"Your next appointment."

"I'll be right with you," Merit said to the woman.

She nodded at Merit and stared at Gilbert.

Merit sat in the conference room across from Mrs. Abigail Ranker. She wore so many diamonds, Merit was tempted to ask her if it was difficult to carry them around on her body.

"I'm sorry Mrs. Ranker. I did not know we had an appointment today. What can I do for you?" Merit asked.

"I just made the appointment with Betty," Mrs. Ranker said. "I wanted to tell you in person that I've decided to end our retainer agreement and hire another law firm."

"May I ask why?" Merit asked.

"I am disturbed about the information I've been seeing on the internet about your firm, Mrs. Ranker said.

"You can't believe everything you read," Merit said.

"My trust is shaken," Mrs. Ranker said.

"I understand, but this could happen to anyone. Your new firm will not be immune to fake news and gossip either," Merit said. "My security team is working on clearing it up. I assure you it's all false."

"My mind is made up. I'm sorry. I think it's best that I move forward elsewhere," Mrs. Ranker said.

"I'm sorry you feel that way, but I will accept your decision. I'll ask Betty to prepare a refund of any escrowed monies left in the retainer account," Merit said.

"Thank you," Mrs. Ranker said and stood to go.

Merit stood and shook her hand.

"You really should be more careful," Mrs. Ranker said.

Merit's mouth dropped open, then she snapped it shut.

29

Merit, Betty, and Ace ordered lunch at Maudie's Tex-Mex Too on South Lamar. The smell of grilling fajitas was so enticing, they had a hard time deciding.

"I want to order the whole menu," Ace said.

Betty and Ace settled on Josie's enchiladas, while Merit ordered a fajita taco salad. Ace was in town from Houston for a three-day weekend. Merit suspected that Betty had called him to come home to cheer her up. Regardless, it was working. Nothing thrilled her heart like the sight of her son's smile.

"I like your t-shirt," Merit said to Ace. "Who is that?"

"It's Jesse Sublett and the Skunks," Ace said.

The TV above the bar showed the headlines between sports events. Betty nodded at Merit to block Ace's view, but it was too late.

"I see it, you two. You think I don't know what's going on in Austin just because I go to school in Houston?" Ace said.

"We know you keep up, Peaches. It's just that I wanted a break from the stress of all the media attention, however brief," Merit said.

"I want you to know, Mom, I never believe a word of it," Ace said.

"Of course not," Betty said. "We all know your Mom is as pure as the day is long."

"The internet news is the worst," Ace said. "I always thought that what was there was mostly true. Now I see I've been played all this time."

"New technology, new problems," Merit said.

"It's been around for a while," Betty said. "P.T. Barnum had the Penny Papers. They were full of gossip and false statements that people believed."

"Like the Barnum and Bailey Circus?" Ace asked.

"Right. There's always been fake news. It just spreads faster with social media," Merit said.

"Have you ever heard of Woodward and Bernstein?" Betty asked.

"No, who is that?" Ace asked.

"They investigated a big case that led to the impeachment and removal from office of Richard Nixon in the early seventies," Betty said.

"We studied it at Rice in my journalism class. Woodward and Bernstein wrote a book about it that was made into a movie. It was called *All the President's Men*," Merit said.

"Really? I never heard of it. We did study about Nixon." Ace said.

"What struck me about the book was how the Washington Post made their reports have two independent sources to confirm information before they would publish it," Betty said.

"Some thought Deep Throat from the book was really a compilation of several sources," Merit said.

"It was still more ethical and unbiased back then," Betty said.

"Now, each person has to figure out everything for themselves. We can't trust just one news source," Merit said.

"They're all just singin' to the choir," Betty said.

"What does that mean? Ace asked.

"It means that people watch the news channels that agree with their belief systems and that reinforces what they already think is true," Merit said. "When the only news you are willing to hear is partisan, you are susceptible to stories that are complete and utter fabrications just because they sing your favorite tune."

"And sex sells, or in Merit's case, scandal," Betty said. "People love a good controversy whether it's true or not."

"Some say there is no trusted media. I search for credible news sources all the time," Merit said.

"I guess we have to see it in person to believe it," Ace said. "Live video."

"Even that can be doctored," Merit said.

"The trust of the innocent is the liar's most useful tool," Betty said.

"Abe Lincoln?" Ace asked.

"Stephen King," Betty said.

30

L.A. and Ash motored along Hollywood and Vine past the Capitol Records Tower and over to Rodeo Drive. L.A. sat in the back of the Escalade.

"I love Los Angeles," L.A. said.

"Much better than Texas," Ash said. "No one there I care to know."

"Except for Buddy Holly, Guy Clark, Lightning Hopkins, Doc Watson, Radney Foster, and The Big Bopper, just to name a few," L.A. said.

Ash didn't respond. *Half of them are dead*, he thought.

L.A. took a phone call from HackerDude while Ash looked for a parking place.

"Nothing open. Want to valet?" Ash asked.

"Just let me out on the corner. I want to get some tailored shirts. If you find a place to park, come back. If not, I'll text you when to pick me up," L.A. said.

Ash frowned and pulled over to the curb. He squealed his tires when he took off, barely missing L.A.'s exit from the back seat.

L.A. scowled at the back of the SUV then continued his phone conversation on the sidewalk outside of Hermes.

"I want to step it up a notch. Let's give Merit Bridges a little more heat," L.A. said.

"How about some type of anonymous interview on YouTube. Create some conspiracy theorist chatter." HackerDude said on the phone.

"You mean like she's in a cult or something?" L.A. said. "I don't think that will work with her. Maybe Scientology, just the word makes people freak out."

"How about something with her old buddy the mayor," HackerDude said.

"That's more like it," L.A. said.

L.A. wrapped up his shopping just in time to head home to his 90210 address and primp for his date. He put on a new black Tom Ford suit with double vents in back and looked in the mirror.

"Tom Ford and music are the only decent things ever to come out of Texas," L.A. said to his reflection."

A few minutes later, Ash picked him up with supermodel Alana already in the car and L.A. climbed into the back with her. Alana wore a slinky short silver dress, the latest runway hit from Alexander McQueen.

"You look lovely tonight, Alana," L.A. said.

She smiled automatically.

Alana and women like her who wanted to see and be seen were L.A.'s specialty. The unspoken arrangement was the same with each one. Look great, don't expect anything romantic, keep quiet about anything personal, and never ever spend the night.

L.A. had not had sex since his brother's incident. His mind was willing, but his body never again responded to the urge that didn't arrive. He had hoped for years that the abstinence would pass. He tried every type of slump buster he could think of including hookers and Viagra. Nothing worked, including his penis.

Little was said as they cut across Beverly Hills and Ash dropped them at the Troubadour on Santa Monica Boulevard. The venue was known for scouting the best bands of the future before the rest of the country took note. The Doors, James Taylor and Elton John flourished there in the early days. In later years, Coldplay, Florence and the Machine, The Red Hot Chili Peppers, and countless others got their foothold in the music biz by walking through the door and doing their thing.

L.A. was a regular and the security guards opened the velvet ropes on the side of the line to allow his passage. L.A. placed his hand on the small of Alana's back. It was the only time he liked being shorter than someone. The status afforded by being seen with the statuesque women he dated added to his power and mystique in L.A.

The hostess showed them to a choice table in the VIP glass room upstairs. They looked down on the crowd moving to the music and sipped Armand de Brignac Rose Champagne. It wasn't the taste L.A. enjoyed as much as being seen with the unmistakable bright pink bottle in his ice bucket. Other A-listers whispered and guessed the designers both Alana and L.A. wore. Several rock stars stopped by their table to shake hands with L.A. He wallowed in the glow of his power and celebrity.

L.A. topped off Alana's glass and they settled in to listen to L.A.'s newest client with a career bloom expected to rival any to date.

While L.A. basked in the limelight, HackerDude downloaded a letter from Val's computer which was written on "The Law Office of Merit Bridges" letterhead. He removed the body of the correspondence, leaving the logo, addressee and signature at the bottom. He then cut and pasted bogus content into the middle of the document and saved the new fake letter as a pdf file.

Next, he created two YouTube videos with a talking head of the mayor holding up the letter from Merit's office. The first had him in cahoots with her and the second had him criticizing her. He then encrypted the entire package and emailed it to L.A. via one of their bogus accounts.

"Pick your poison, L.A.," HackerDude said.

Later that night, L.A. looked through the footage from HackerDude and made his selection for posting on YouTube. He liked the one with the mayor in cahoots. There was nothing that made a politician run faster than rubbing up against someone in disfavor.

The video showed the mayor's talking head and hands holding the letter on Merit's letterhead, pointing to the signature and then throwing his head back and laughing like a character in a bad B movie.

The movement of the mayor's lips did not match the voice over, but that was irrelevant to the goal.

L.A. uploaded it to YouTube.

Next, he clicked over to another program showing traffic stats on his fake sites. He analyzed the past week based on what had been posted, then saw a huge spike at the end of the graph.

"Where is that coming from?" L.A. asked himself.

He refreshed the information, clicked through the program, and saw that the YouTube video was already being watched by hundreds of people. The reason was a vast number of conspiracy sites had copied the talking head and added their own explanations. It all linked back to the original bogus page.

L.A. watched the numbers a while longer and laughed. By that time, it was 3 a.m. in Los Angeles, 5 a.m. in Austin. In Trump style, L.A. posted bogus tweets about Merit's illegal and questionable activities and linked them to the faux page. The fake tweets boosted the views on the blog site even further.

31

Merit and Ag sat at Polvo's on South First Street drinking top shelf margaritas, munching tortilla chips, and listening to Los Lonely Boys on the sound system. Almost everyone in the restaurant was moving in their seats to the Tejano beat. Ag went to the sauce bar and refilled their bowl with chipotle salsa, Merit's favorite.

Merit opened the menu and studied the choices. She could smell onions grilling in the kitchen.

When Ag came back to the table, he took an envelope from his pocket and gave it to Merit. She opened it to find two tickets to the Lyle Lovett concert at the Paramount Theatre. Reckless Kelly was listed as the opening act.

"Peace offering?" Merit asked.

"I guess," Ag said. "You can take anyone of any age you want."

"Nothing says I'm hurtin' like the moan of a lonesome guitar," Merit said.

"I'm sorry," Ag said. "I have no right to judge you."

"You can't stay mad at me," Merit laughed. "Not while everyone else is out to get me."

Merit took a long sip of her margarita and stopped just short of brain freeze. She looked pained.

"We'll get to the bottom of this, Merit. Whoever it is can't hide forever," Ag said.

"Maybe they're tired of it. I haven't seen anything in a couple of days," Merit said.

Both Ag's and Merit's phones buzzed.

"Oh no," Ag said looking at his phone.

"What?" Merit asked.

"It's a text from Betty to both of us," Ag said. "She says she doesn't want you to be caught off guard."

"What now?" Merit said. She picked up her phone and clicked the link Betty had attached to the text.

Several people at other tables around them looked at their phones, began to whisper and gestured at Merit.

The news was on a site called Texas Politics Insider and it showed a cartoonish picture of the mayor holding up a letter from Merit's office. The letter showed dollar amounts and an alleged list of donors that had contributed to the mayor's last campaign. The list was Merit's best paying clients.

Merit began to panic. She tried to catch her breath and choke out a defense.

"I've never raised money for Mayor Taylor," Merit said. "But that list could only have come from my office."

"I'll give Parson at Tech Security a head's up. This has to stop," Ag said.

"Please, and soon," Merit said.

"Let's get you out of here," Ag said and threw some cash on the table.

♪

Merit sat on her patio drinking a glass of Texas' Hye Meadow Winery Montepulciano, looking at the view, and wondering how she had lost so much control over her life. Her iPhone buzzed and vibrated and she picked it up but didn't accept the call.

"I can't take anything more today," she said to the phone.

She saw Ace's picture on the screen, so she hit the green icon.

"Hey, Mom," Ace said.

Merit let out a breath.

"Hi, Peaches. It's good to hear your voice. How are things in Houston?" Merit asked.

"What's wrong, Mom?" Ace asked.

"You know me too well. Long day, nothing for you to worry about."

For once, Merit was glad that Ace's school was not in Austin. The last thing he needed was to deal with the gossip and innuendo on a daily basis.

"Can I help?" Ace asked.

"It's 'may I help', and just talking to you is already making it better," Merit said.

He'd been forced grow up much faster than he should have when his father died. Merit wasn't about to give him the job of propping her up on top of all he'd gone through.

"How's school?" Merit said.

"Pretty good this week. I wrote a paper for my Social Studies class about fake news. There was a story on National Public Radio and I used that as research in the quotes," Ace said.

"Wow. I guess you were listening when we talked about it with Betty," Merit said.

"I listen, sometimes," Ace laughed.

"Glad to hear it. Tell me about the paper," Merit said.

"The NPR story looks at what it's like when readers are duped by fake news as opposed to the media trying to sort out what's fake and what's not. So, I went with that angle and applied it to my age group," Ace said.

"I'm impressed. Tell me more," Merit said.

"Well, the NPR story was about how researchers at Stanford's grad school of education looked at a year of online news sources to see how well students could evaluate info," Ace said.

Merit sat up straight in her chair.

"The researchers said they were shocked at how many students failed at the credibility test of the news as presented. Just because it was in social media and students know all about that, they thought students would know better. It was just the opposite."

"Really?"

"Yep. Middle school students can't tell adverts from articles and believed that sponsored content is real news. High school students didn't do much better. Most of them accepted all photographs as real. And, they can't tell the difference between real and fake news sources on Facebook."

"That's surprising," Merit said.

"I know. Most college students don't think that there's bias in a tweet from an activist group. Even Stanford students couldn't identify the difference between mainstream and fringe sources."

"You mean all the planted or biased material looked real to these kids?" Merit asked.

"Exactly. Hardly anyone checked, not even on really doctored pictures. They just believed it and even spread it round," Ace said.

"That's discouraging," Merit said.

"Worst part is, once they believe it, it's true in their minds," Ace said. "Even if they later see evidence controverting it, they tend to believe the original news. Or worse, do something based on the info when it's not even true," Ace said.

"The only way society can get around this is to educate people on how easy it is to post fake news and how irresponsible it is to share it without checking it out first," Merit said.

"Even the most educated wonder about a story that goes out on social media," Ace said.

"Right. There's a saying in the law that you can't un-ring a bell," Merit said, frowned, and took a long sip of her wine.

32

Kim Wan sat in the Travis County Courthouse at the defense table in Criminal Court Number Three with Davey beside him. Davey looked shrunken and pale. His pants were held on by tightly cinching in his belt. The waistband ruffled around his waist like a fluted pie crust.

Merit sat in the back of the courtroom. She made eye contact with Kim Wan, but did not inject herself into the proceedings. She was nervous for Davey. He had been in jail a long time for such a young man. To be accused of killing his father must be unbearable. Her heart went out to him.

Directly behind Kim Wan and Davey sat Reverend Hightower in his customary black duster and black slacks. It appeared he had pressed the outfit for the occasion as his Nehru collar stood up around his neck. His beard was trimmed short.

Ash Joyner slipped into the back of the courtroom and pressed the button on his tape recorder hidden under a *Texas Monthly* magazine.

"All stand," the bailiff sang out.

Judge Crow entered, looking striking and powerful in his black robe, took the bench, perched in his chair, and made a motion with his hands for all to sit. The judge nodded at Prosecutor Jason Ellsworth.

The prosecutor stood on cue and began his argument. "Your Honor, bail is still out of the question. Mr. Bell, or Mr. Nolan, as he currently calls himself, is as much a flight risk as ever. Now that we know who his father is, we know that his father is deceased. We have not seen any sign of his mother, and the University of Texas has made no move to allow him back into school. Other than his attorney, he appears to know no one of substance in Austin."

"What say you, Mr. Thibodeaux?" Judge Crow asked.

Kim Wan stood, looked at Davey and Reverend Hightower, then addressed the court.

"Your Honor, now that it has been established that Davey Nolan is related to Liam Nolan, a friend of the family has come forth to assist with bail and supervision. Reverend Hightower of the St. John's Men's Shelter was Liam Nolan's NA sponsor and friend of recent years. He housed Liam Nolan when he first returned to Austin, assisted in helping him maintain sobriety, and continued to befriend him up until his unfortunate death. Reverend Hightower is willing to take Davey into the living quarters at the facility, provide food and shelter, and monitor his whereabouts until the murder trial."

Prosecutor Ellsworth jumped up from his chair.

"Your Honor, this man is practically homeless himself. What guarantee do we have that he will keep tabs on the boy? Murder is a serious charge."

Judge Crow's eyes moved over to Kim Wan with a question mark in them.

"Mr. Thibodeaux?" Judge Crow asked.

"The case against my client is purely circumstantial, Your Honor. Reverend Hightower is the brother of Judge Warren Hightower of the district court in this very building. Reverend Hightower's shelter is funded by the Austin Charity Umbrella and has been in its current location for over twelve years. Valuable work is done there on behalf of the disenfranchised of the city. Reverend Hightower is here if you'd like to question him," Kim Wan said.

Kim Wan turned and motioned to Reverend Hightower to stand. The tall, thin, black figure uncurled from the bench looking like a raven ready for flight.

"Reverend Hightower," Judge Crow said. "Are you willing to monitor this young man and make sure he shows up for trial?"

Kim Wan nodded at Reverend Hightower, giving him the cue to speak.

"Yes Sir. I'll make sure he's fed, clothed, and clean for trial," Reverend Hightower said.

"I'm inclined to allow Mr. Nolan to go with the Reverend. From what I understand, you have no finger prints or other physical evidence making your case mostly circumstantial," Judge Crow said.

"Your Honor," Prosecutor Ellsworth said. "At least place some financial burden on the defendant to appear and make him wear an ankle monitor."

"If you'll let me run my courtroom, Mr. Ellsworth, I was just about to do that. Bail is set at one hundred thousand dollars, cash or bond, and the defendant must remain in the custody of Reverend Hightower until and during trial, and wear an ankle monitor at all times."

Ellsworth smiled. Davey deflated. Reverend Hightower looked confused.

The judge slammed the gavel and looked at the bailiff.

"Call the next case."

♪

Merit and Kim Wan met with Davey in the attorney interview room just outside the courtroom.

"I don't have a hundred thousand dollars," Davey said. "And what's a bond?"

"A bond of twenty percent of bail is placed with the court by a bail bondsman who guarantees you will appear. In your case, the bondsman will guarantee the money," Merit said. "If you don't show up, they have to pay the full amount to the court."

"Why would they do that?" Davey asked.

"Someone has to put up some collateral for you to entice the insurers to pay your bond. If you don't show, the collateral is taken by the bail bondsman and sold to cover the cost of the payment to the court," Kim Wan said.

"Collateral, like a house or car?" Davey asked.

"Right," Merit said.

"You know I don't have that either. This is like no bail at all. Why did we have Reverend Hightower come in here if I can't get out? He doesn't have money, does he?"

"No, he's on a shoestring budget. But you do have assets. You are presently the only heir to Liam Nolan's estate," Merit said.

"I have a friend who's a bail bondsman. I think he will take Merit's pledge from the estate until the probate is complete," Kim Wan said.

"If you don't show, Davey, I'll be forced to liquidate the estate and pay the court. It's barely worth the hundred thousand I'll pledge, but Kim Wan will call in the favor with his bondsman if you want to assure us you will show up and stand trial," Merit said.

"Of course. Get me out, please," Davey said.

What am I getting myself into? Merit thought.

Merit and Kim Wan exchanged mirrored looks.

33

The day after Davey was released on bail, he was in Merit's office first thing for pancakes with Betty.

When Merit arrived, she smelled the butter, and went into the break room.

"We don't have an appointment, Davey," Merit said.

Davey pushed a big slice of pancake into his mouth and chugged downed half a glass of orange juice. He took a swipe at his mouth with a napkin but missed half the syrup on his chin.

"I want a will. I don't know what's going to happen to me, but if something bad hits, I want you to finish what we started," Davey said.

"Nothing is going to happen to you," Merit said. "How are things going at the shelter? Don't they feed you there?"

"Yes, but Betty's a better cook," Davey said.

Betty beamed.

"I want a will and I want it now. Liam waited and look what happened," Davey said.

"I'll write a temporary will for you today, but I can't write a proper will for you now. It takes planning and time. There are tax ramifications and all sorts of clauses that require consideration. Come back in a few days and we'll go through it all. Okay?" Merit asked.

"Okay, but this temporary will can work if something happens?" Davey asked. "I feel like something is going to happen."

"Yes, it will be binding the minute you sign it, witnesses sign it, and Betty notarizes it. But nothing is going to happen. Just stay at the shelter and keep your head down," Merit said.

"Okay. Good," Davey said.

"Who do you want to give your assets to?" Merit said.

"What did Liam want?" Davey asked.

"He had several charities in mind. But remember, we're not talking about a lot of money here. Once you pay Kim Wan and the probate fees, there's not much left to bequeath," Merit said.

"Ok, use the charities Liam liked and add The High School for the Performing Arts in Hyde Park on Forty-Fifth Street. Make sure it goes to the music department," Davey said.

"Wait here and drink some more orange juice," Betty said to Davey.

Merit and Betty walked down the hall to Merit's office.

"Hasn't he become the demanding client. Now you're stocking breakfast supplies for him? Orange juice?" Merit asked.

"I'll bring you some tea. Want orange juice, too?" Betty asked.

Merit rolled her eyes. She turned toward her office causing her blond ponytail to flip.

"Fill out the short form will and I'll tweak it. Try to round up a couple of witnesses from the office down the hall," Merit said over her shoulder.

"On it," Betty said.

"Also, make an appointment for him to come back for a consultation regarding his longer will, please," Merit said. "I hope he has a calendar."

"Speaking of calendar, you have a meeting in an hour," Betty said.

"Like I don't know that," Merit said as she turned into her office door.

34

The next day, Merit called Betty from the speaker phone in her office.

"Could you have everyone in the conference room in an hour? We need to make a list of possible suspects from our client list for Detective Chaplain," Merit said.

"On it," Betty said.

Down the street in the Warehouse District, L.A. listened to the conversation in Merit's office.

"Damn. Can't you meet in your office?" L.A. said to the computer.

He had not found a way to bug Merit's conference room. Unfortunately, most of her bigger meetings were in that room and not her office.

L.A. picked up the phone and texted HackerDude.

I need to get into that conference room! L.A. thought.

When Merit went into the meeting, Betty had a cup of tea at the head of the table for her. The staff of Betty, Val and Mai, plus Ag were sitting around the table. Each member had a printout of the firm's clients and pink and yellow highlighters at the ready. Empty napkins with crumbs were beside the lists.

A plate of Betty's lemon squares with chocolate drizzle was sitting in the middle of the conference table. The treat was half gone.

"Kick us off please, Betty," Merit said. "I better get one of these while I can."

She picked up a lemon square, took a bite, looked at Betty, and moaned.

Betty smiled.

"Okay. What you have before you is a printout of the firm's present day clients and those going back three years. The yellow highlighter means maybe and the pink highlighter means it goes on the list for Chaplain," Betty said.

"We don't want to give him the entire client list," Ag said. "It would take him too long to check out the suspects. We need to whittle it down to the most likely persons to hold a grudge against Merit and the firm."

"Let's work through each name and we'll all comment on any issues we may be aware of," Betty said.

Betty called the first name and the group began the laborious task of working through hundreds of names and placing them on the suspect, maybe, and no-way lists. Top of the suspect list was a nasty developer who had tried to put a high-rise on Lake Travis property next to the Oasis. Merit had represented the Lake Travis Preservation Association against him and won. A lot of yelling in public had ensued. The county ruling was under review and accusations were flying about the rights of property owners versus the rights of citizens.

L.A. Baron and Louellen Bell were not on the lists, as they were not clients and were new to the scene. Davey did not make the list because he had no motive. Liam did not make the list because he was dead.

The staff worked well into the night. By the time they wrapped up the work, the lemon squares were all gone. Merit stayed after and looked at the list one last time. She tried to use her Spidey sense to see if any name popped out or gave her pause. No name on the list jumped out at her.

"I hope this works," Merit said.

35

Louellen Bell walked on four inch heels into the Law Office of Merit Bridges and addressed the receptionist.

"I want to see Lawyer Bridges," Louellen said.

"Do you have an appointment?" Mai asked.

"No, but she'll see me. I'm Davey Ray Bell's mother," Louellen said.

Betty came out of her office.

"I'll handle this," Betty said to Mai who promptly scooted down the hall to the break room.

"Who are you?" Louellen said.

"I'm Merit's office manager. Please have a seat and I'll see if she can work you into her schedule," Betty said.

Betty mumbled all the way down the hallway to Merit's office, came back a few minutes later, and escorted Louellen to the conference room. She did not offer coffee.

Merit took a deep breath and sat at the head of the conference table although Louellen was seated several chairs down in the middle.

"How may I help you?" Merit asked.

"I'm here about Liam's estate. I have claims just like Davey does," Louellen said.

"Have you seen Davey?" Merit asked.

"Yes, I just saw him at Reverend Hightower's shelter," Louellen said.

"How do you feel about your son living in a shelter?" Merit asked.

"That's none of your business. I'm here about the estate, and since you are the administrator, you have to address my claims," Louellen said.

"Yes, but you must have proof of your claims. What are you asserting as your rights in the estate?" Merit asked.

"I was common law married to Liam and I wrote part of his songs, especially *Fever Stomp*," Louellen said.

"That's quite a claim," Merit said. "The Texas statute to establish common law marriage is very specific. Do you have proof or have you established a timeline of your marriage? Did you have joint bank accounts or did Liam hold you out publicly as his wife?"

"Yes, some of that," Louellen said.

"I'll need to see what you have, or you could file a claim with the probate court. Either way, they will have the final say on whether your claim has merit," Merit said.

"I'm going to get a lawyer," Louellen said.

"A lawyer is a very good idea. Please have your representative contact me. Here's my card with my email and phone numbers," Merit said.

"You just don't spend any of my money until I get my claim in," Louellen said and stomped out of the room.

Betty, standing outside the door, escorted Louellen out of the office.

She could start a fight in an empty house, Betty thought.

36

M erit pulled up Google Alerts on her computer.

"Time to check on my reputation, what's left of it," Merit said to the screen.

A new fake news story had been published and was circulating through the suspicious sites Merit had seen the week before. She had been making a list of them for Austin Tech.

"Bridges breaches confidence of major client. Gives inside information to her friend Red Thallon," Merit read aloud.

The article went on to give details of events that never occurred and that were impossible for Merit to deny without attracting further attention. If she went public, she would garner scrutiny, if she remained silent, no one was out there defending her and her good name.

Merit popped up Facebook and went through each post and opened the drop-down menu to *Report Post*. She clicked through everything she could find about her that was fake, reporting as she went.

Next, Merit drafted a letter to Facebook and attached screenshot examples of the various fake news posts that she'd found. She included a list of the faux sites that had been identified by Tech Security. The letter stated that while she could not respond to the various posts without further damage to her reputation, she expected

Facebook to investigate and make sure the pages were legitimate. She stopped short of threatening to bring legal action.

It was a weak gesture, but it was all she could think of to do. She was so angry her hands shook as she attached the letter to an email and hit SEND.

♪

Betty came in with a stack of files. She looked at Merit's face.

"What's happened now?" Betty asked. "You look so low you couldn't jump off a dime."

"Same ol', same ol'. Lies and more lies," Merit said.

"Let me see," Betty said.

"They're asserting that Tony's suicide may have involved foul play," Merit said. "The gist is I may have had something to do with it."

"What a yellow-bellied scum sucker thing to say," Betty said. "Can't even use a gun on the cowards when they're hiding out in the weeds of social media."

"I need to sue somebody," Merit said.

Betty looked at the latest fake news over Merit's shoulder.

"Pitiful," Betty said.

Merit clicked over to another site and pulled up several tort cases on defamation of character.

"I'm tired of this. These statements clearly meet the standard for libel. They are published, false, injurious and unprivileged," Merit said.

"Outrageous," Betty said.

"I could clearly sue the publisher if I could find out who he or she is," Merit said.

"How are Ag and Chaplain doing with the investigation?" Betty asked.

"It's going nowhere. Every search leads to a dead end or another one of these fake companies. It's like chasing a ghost according to Chaplain," Merit said. "It's clear now that it's an orchestrated attack on my character. Not random."

"There has to be a way to find these jerks," Betty said.

"Set another meeting with Parsons from Tech Security for tomorrow. I'll take this meeting alone," Merit said.

♪

Later that day, Merit placed a call to her mentor and father figure, Woody Woodward in Houston. Merit composed herself while she waited for Woody's receptionist to locate him.

"Merit, you sound upset, dear. What's wrong? Is Ace all right?" Woody said.

"Ace is fine. Woody, I have no control over my life anymore," Merit said. "Everywhere I turn someone is posting or printing or announcing something about me that just isn't true."

"Is this gossip or intentional?" Woody asked.

"I'm under attack," Merit said. "Someone is out to get me and I'm not being paranoid."

"Have you gone to the police?" Woody asked.

"Ag has filed complaints and talked to a detective at APD, but it's like chasing a ghost in the machine. There's no one to accuse," Merit said.

"Calm down, dear. Tell me what set you off," Woody said.

"I found some gossip a while back that's been increasingly malicious. A few minutes ago, I found a story about one of my clients that only I knew about. The client would never reveal it. The story points directly at me and my firm as the leak," Merit said.

"Is this a major client?" Woody asked.

"Yes, I'm on the board of directors of their company and serve as their chief council. It couldn't be much worse, only it is," Merit said.

"How so," Woody asked.

"A friend of mine at the local TV station, Red Thallon, received some confidential documents on my firm letterhead about the client. Only, they're fake," Merit said.

"The client must know they're fake," Woody said.

"Yes, but they are looking at me sideways," Merit said.

"Ah, a trust issue," Woody said.

"Yes, and they've set a meeting to discuss it with me," Merit said. "What do I do?"

"You must not appear to be disheveled or lose your composure. You must become the best actress you can. Be steadfast and hold your ground. You can't control what the client does, but you can control yourself. Maintain your pride," Woody said.

Merit straightened her backbone and sat up in her chair.

"Okay, how do I do that?" Merit said.

♪

Merit entered the corporate offices of Global Financial, LLC in the Arboretum in North Austin. Global had been one of her biggest clients since she left the Houston firm and she and Betty had opened the Law Office of Merit Bridges. She'd handled numerous transactions for them over the years, most in the millions of dollars. They'd asked her to become a member of the board about three years ago, and she had served in that capacity conscientiously and with pride.

"I'm here for a meeting with Carl Fordman," she told the receptionist who sat behind a desk so tall all that could be seen was her head.

"Right this way, he's expecting you," the receptionist said, standing and moving down a long corridor.

Merit followed her slowly as if walking to the gallows. She was shown into a conference room with glass windows that looked out over statues of granite cows grazing near a man-made pond. She didn't have long to wait until Fordman joined her.

"Hello, Carl. I thought the board would be here," Merit said.

"They've asked me to handle the matter since it is a delicate one," Fordman said.

"The matter?" Merit asked.

"Merit, you know we have worked well together for some time. We've enjoyed that relationship and expected many more years together," Fordman said.

"As have I," Merit said.

"In the current climate in Austin, we can't afford to have even a hint of scandal surrounding the board. It is very hard to wash away any assertion of impropriety," Fordman said.

"Just spit it out, Carl. What are you trying to say?" Merit said.

"Remember Lance Armstrong?" Fordman said.

"Of course," Merit said.

"He almost took down Livestrong with his doping scandal," Fordman said.

"But he was doping. I've done nothing wrong," Merit said.

"He stepped aside for the benefit of the organization. We need you to do the same," Fordman said. "The board has already voted."

"They forced him out for cause. You've admitted that my work is more than satisfactory on many occasions. This is unfair," Merit said.

"It's a very difficult call," Fordman said.

Merit saw that it was too late to save the relationship. She thought of Woody and sat up in her chair. *Backbone, not wishbone,* she thought.

"Of course, Carl," Merit said. "I hope at a future date, when all this is cleared up, that you'll reconsider."

She seemed poised, but she was screaming inside with no way to battle the invisible foe that was stealing her life.

37

Betty brought the snail mail into Merit's office along with a cup of tea with milk for Merit.

"This is interesting," Betty said as she pointed to the top document. It was on a report clipped to an envelope.

Merit took a sip of tea, looked at the report and pulled it away from the paperclip.

"ASCAP?" Merit asked.

"Val has been sorting hundreds of these," Merit said.

"Not postmarked from Japan," Betty said.

"Japan? How did we get it?" Merit asked.

Merit flipped the envelope over and looked at the return address.

"Looks like it was forwarded by the post office from Liam Nolan's former address," Betty said.

"Let's get Val in here," Merit said.

Betty picked up the phone and spoke into the interoffice com system. A few minutes later, Val walked in with a file about an inch thick.

"These are all ASCAP for this calendar year," Val said.

"What does ASCAP stand for?" Betty asked.

"American Society of Composer, Authors and Publishers," Merit said.

"Learn something new every day," Betty said.

"Anything from Japan in there?" Merit asked.

"Nope," Val said.

"Does that mean Liam didn't sell in Japan before this?" Betty asked.

"I don't know," Val said. "How does it work with foreign rights?"

"When ASCAP works are performed in a foreign country, that country's performing rights society tracks the performances, collects the license fees from the local music users and then forwards the royalties earned to ASCAP in this country for distribution. We in the U.S., having reciprocal agreements, do the same here and send the data and fees to the appropriate society in foreign countries."

"How could Liam sell music in Japan?" Val asked.

"Anyone in the world can pick up the music and play it. When they do, a royalty is due to the rights holder or holders," Merit said.

"Question is, why did Japan start listening to Liam's music now?" Betty said.

"Exactly. Check the file, Val, and check the history of rights on this song," Merit said.

She handed the report to Val who scanned down the page to the title.

"*Fever Stomp*? That's an oldie," Val said.

"If I remember correctly, Louellen Bell said she helped Liam write that song," Merit said.

♪

Merit opened her email and reviewed the memo that Val had prepared and sent covering the Japanese royalties on *Fever Stomp*. She googled around for an understanding of the terminology related to song copyrights, then pulled up JASRAC, the Japanese society responsible for collecting royalties and sending them to the United States to ASCAP.

How does this all fit together? Merit thought. *Why would this song suddenly start paying off?*

She opened Liam Nolan's online account at ASCAP and clicked around the page. It took her a while to get the layout of the site, but once she did, she was able to research several of his songs that had small sums trickling in. She found the title registration database. It appeared that several different music publishers had registered some of the songs, mostly taking fifty percent. Liam himself had registered some of the songs and kept one hundred percent.

Once she understood where the money came from, she clicked on *Fever Stomp*. It appeared that the publisher, Allan Roeder, had registered the song. Merit recalled a list of various publishing deals on one of Val's spreadsheets, and the name Roeder was vaguely familiar.

The registration showed Liam's name, the name of the song, *Fever Stomp*; the genre, rock; and fifty percent royalty to the publisher, Allan Roeder. The mailing address led to the publisher and monies to the publisher's account. It didn't show everyone who had rights in the song, but it appeared that the fifty-percent left for Liam was sent to Baron Entertainment Enterprises in Los Angeles.

"If the money was going to Baron, why wasn't a check for Liam's cut being sent onto his estate?" Merit wondered.

She typed up her research and sent it to Val in an email for him to use in checking through Liam's accounting to see if they had missed any payments. She also included a screenshot of the registration page for *Fever Stomp*. Her armpits prickled ever so slightly as she hit SEND.

"We'll get to the bottom of this," Merit said aloud.

Later that night, a few blocks away in the Warehouse District, Baron watched the screen on his computer with increasing dismay. He was reading through the surveillance reports from Val's laptop and saw the memo from Merit asking for the ASCAP research.

She's onto the song in Japan, Baron thought. *Damn.*

L.A. Took one of his burner phones out of his desk.

I was hoping to save this for later, but here goes, L.A. thought.

L.A. dialed Louellen's number and spoke with her for a few short minutes.

He hit end call and put his feet up on his desk.

"Take that, Bridges!" he said.

38

Louellen Bell entered the Mean Eyed Cat on Fifth Street and located L.A. in a dark booth in the back of the bar wearing a Jimmie Vaughan gimme cap low on his forehead. As Louellen moved through the tables and chairs the juke box flipped a forty-five onto the turntable and played 'Broke Down Dreams' by Erick Willis. L.A. closed his eyes and seemed to soak in the tune.

Louellen looked through the window at the three-hundred-year-old Texas Live Oak with her boyfriend sitting beneath it on the patio.

"Where's your buddy?" L.A. asked without rising to pull out her chair.

Louellen stood for a moment waiting, then dropped down into the seat with a thud.

"Oh, he's around," she said.

Someone killed the juke box and The Band in Black returned to the stage for their last set of 'God Bless Johnny Cash'.

"It's dark in here. Not exactly your kind of place, I don't imagine," Louellen said.

"Any place with music is my kind of place. The darkness is the point," L.A. said.

The waitress came over.

"What's your pleasure?" the waitress asked.

"What are you drinking?" Louellen said.

171

"The 'Drink Named Sue'; it's usually vodka with citrus. I substituted gin," L.A. said.

"I'll have a beer," Louellen told the waitress. "Anything on draft."

L.A. paused while the waitress cleared the next table.

"What's up?" Louellen asked.

"It's time for you to turn up the heat on Merit Bridges," L.A. said.

"I've already told her Liam and I were common law married. That ought to keep her busy for a while," Louellen said.

"Her investigator will have that sorted out in no time with your checkered past and trail of tears," L.A. said.

"I don't know what else I can throw her way?" Louellen said.

"Let's go after her law license," L.A. said.

"Good one. How?" Louellen asked.

"I've had one of my associates email some forms to you that need to be filed at the State Bar of Texas. You can fill them out, sign them, and scan them back in or snail mail them over to the Bar," L.A. said.

"Sounds easy enough. What do I say?" Louellen said.

"Tell them she's not fairly representing the interests of all parties. Say she's refused to hear your claims against the estate. Play the mom card about Davey's pitiful situation and how she's not helping to alleviate your pain." L.A. said.

"Well, she's not listening to me. She's not trying to help at all," Louellen said.

"Right, just be your usual friendly self," L.A. said.

Betty brought the mail and a cup of tea for Merit to her office.

"Darlin', this is going to be tough to take," Betty said.

"What now? Merit asked.

"There are two upsetting things in the mail today," Betty said.

Betty pulled a document off the top of the stack and placed it before Merit.

"Louellen's petition through her new attorney to the probate court. It says she was common law married to Liam and she wants half of the estate," Merit said. "She's trying to take money from her own son."

"Shameful," Betty said.

"We knew this was coming. What else?" Merit asked.

Betty pulled a thick letter attached to several documents and placed it on top of the stack.

"Louellen has filed a complaint with the State Bar of Texas alleging mishandling of funds and bias in administering Liam's probate," Betty said.

Merit's eyes got wide and she read the letter and complaint.

"Says there's a hearing on the twenty-fourth," Merit said.

"You'll need to prepare a defense. Who do you want to hire to represent you?" Betty asked.

"She's asking that I be disbarred or suspended," Merit said.

"Bitch," Betty said.

Red Thallon stood at her raised desk in the news room at Austin9Online. She clicked around the internet as she spoke into the microphone of her mobile phone. A photo of Merit and her name were displayed on the screen.

"I'm looking at all this fake news about you now," Red said.

She paused to listen.

"Yes, it is horrible. Some of these participants may have been knowingly complicit while others are just useful idiots," Red said and paused again.

"They only need to sow doubt, not prove that the news is true," Red said.

Pause.

"I'm trying to help, but the speed and coordination of these efforts allows online news to outcompete traditional news organizations for an audience. The playing field isn't level," Red said.

Pause.

"I've tried to track the servers too, but they have purposefully stripped identifying information and transport headers from electronic mail. This stalker has almost perfectly anonymized these messages. It is relatively simple to send anonymous communications while making it difficult for victims, providers, and law enforcement to identify the person responsible for transmitting harassing or threating info," Red said.

Pause.

"Thousands of botnets, and teams of paid human trolls or networks of websites and social media accounts can amplify this crap across the internet faster that we can keep up," Red said.

Pause.

"That's not a word I've heard you use before," Red said.

39

At Merit's request, Ag headed back to Llano for another fact-finding mission on the Bell case. He tuned in some travelling music by James McMurtry.

Ag's goal was to find out more about Louellen Bell and her involvement with Liam Nolan. Who did what to whom, where, and why?

When he arrived in Llano, he started where he'd left off on the last trip at the County Clerk's office and checked again under the name Pounder – Louellen's husband after Davey was born. He made a note of the date of their divorce and checked further to see if Louellen had been subsequently married to anyone else.

"No takers," Ag said to himself.

Ag googled the local bar scene on his phone and found five Llano area hangouts that looked promising. He narrowed the search further by eliminating two nicer pubs with food service and one dive bar that fit the bill but was new. The remaining two honkey-tonks looked equally tawdry and suspect. One appeared to be more of a dance hall.

Ag went to the first, Joe's Balls. Inside, he saw that it was mostly pool tables with a small bar and dance floor. Robert Earl Keen was playing on the sound system. No band.

The place was empty except for two local looking alcoholics at the end of the bar. Ag decided to take a shot at the bartender. From the name on his shirt, it was Joe himself.

"Hey, I'll have whatever's on draft," Ag said.

"Comin' right up," Joe said.

"Are you the owner Joe?" Ag asked.

"That's me," Joe said.

He sat the beer before Ag, no napkin, no coaster, and said, "Three bucks."

Ag took out his wallet and laid a fiver on the bar.

"Keep the change," Ag said.

Joe nodded and started wiping down the peeling bar.

Ag bided his time and sipped some foam.

"Anything else?" Joe asked on his next pass at Ag's end of the bar.

"Information, if you have it," Ag said.

Joe grunted.

"I'm looking into some background for a probate in Austin and I want to find out about Louellen Bell," Ag said.

"I got nothin' for ya'," Joe said.

"Does that mean you don't know anything or you're not sayin'?" Ag asked.

Joe sized Ag up for a minute.

"I don't know much. You might try over at Two-Steppers. It's a dance hall on the outskirts of town," Joe said. "It's been there forever."

"That was my next stop," Ag said. "Anyone in particular that might be helpful over there?"

"There's a waitress that rented a room from Louellen Bell for a while back in the day. Her name is Daisy," Joe said.

Ag downed the last of his beer and threw another fiver on the bar.

"Thanks, man," Ag said.

"Take a look at Two-Steppers at the wall by the men's room," Joe said.

♪

Ag parked in the caliche lot at Two-Steppers and looked at the sign on the door. He checked his watch. It would be thirty minutes before they opened at five o'clock.

He took out his file and started putting dates on a legal pad with notations beside them. First was Davey's date of birth. Next was Louellen's marriage to Pounder. He filled in the most likely dates Liam had been in the area to play music with question marks beside them. Next, he added the dates Liam bought and sold his Llano property. He scribbled a few notes in the margins and added a list of questions at the bottom so he wouldn't forget to verify other data.

Ag looked up to see the *DAMN RIGHT WE'RE OPEN* blue neon sign turn on in the window and packed up his paperwork. He went in and stood at the door until his eyes adjusted. The room was a vast warehouse space with a huge dance floor and a stage in one corner with a drum set and a couple of empty guitar stands. The music system was playing a Delbert McClinton tune Ag couldn't identify. A long bar took up an entire wall across from the stage. It looked and smelled like fresh cut cedar. Ag took a seat on the end closest to the men's room.

"What'll it be?" asked the bartender with no name tag.

"Whatever's on draft," Ag said.

Tagless pulled a beer into a frosty mug and slid it over to Ag. Ag handed him a ten spot and took a sip. When Tagless brought his change, Ag said, "Keep an eye on this for me, will you?"

Tagless nodded and Ag went to the men's room. He walked past photos of Joe Ely, Angela Strehli, Charlie Sexton, W.C. Clark, and Kinky Freidman.

When he came out, he paused to look at the framed pictures hanging all the way down the wall to the women's restroom. The photos were faded, most of the frames rusty, except for the wooden ones. Pics of Texas music greats Willie Nelson, Waylon Jennings, W.C. Clark, Butch Hancock, Jimmie Dale Gilmore, Van Wilks, and Jimmie Vaughan were in the mix.

Next, Ag saw what appeared to be Liam and used his flashlight app on his iPhone to take a closer look. Sure enough, it was Liam on the stage across the room playing his guitar in front of a full band with three female singers standing behind him. One was Louellen.

"Whew," Ag whistled. "No wonder. She was a knockout."

He took a photo of the picture with his phone and then did a close-up of the top half and bottom half. There was a date at the bottom right, but he couldn't make it out.

He walked down the row of pictures but didn't see anything else related to his research and went back to the bar.

"You think I might ask you a couple of questions about this picture?" Ag asked Tagless.

"Maybe," Tagless said.

"I'm researching the heirs of Liam Nolan. See he's here in this photo." Ag held up the phone.

"Yeah, I knew Liam way back. He played here a lot when we first opened," Tagless said.

"I was wondering if you ever saw him with this woman," Ag asked and pointed to Louellen.

"Yeah, they hooked up for a while when she was singin' back up in his band," Tagless said. "After they broke up, she shacked up for a while at her Mama's old place with Black Masters. This guy," Tagless said and pointed to the bass guitar player in the photo.

"Had her parents already passed away by then?" Ag asked.

"Yeah, her Mama would never let her bring home a guy. Louellen had the house by then. When they split up, Masters moved to Austin and claimed common law marriage. I heard he tried to take some of her inheritance," Tagless said.

"Did he win?" Ag asked.

"Never heard," Tagless said. "There's a picture of Louellen and Black over by the office."

"There?" Ag pointed to the door beyond the bathrooms.

"Yep," Tagless said.

"Mind if I take a picture of the photo?" Ag asked.

"Everybody takes pictures of that wall. Besides, you already took one without askin'," Tagless said.

"Guess I did. Thanks," Ag said and left the ten on the bar.

He went to the very back of the room and found the picture of Louellen sitting on the lap of a grizzly fellow who resembled the bass player. Ag snapped a shot of it and repeated the same close-ups top and bottom.

"Gotcha!" Ag said to Louellen in the pic.

He saluted Tagless on his way to the door.

40

On a beautiful spring evening, Merit and Ace exited her BMW at the entrance to the Long Center for the Performing Arts between Riverside Drive and Barton Springs Road. Merit wore a baby blue lace and tulle tea length gown with a sweetheart neckline and plunging back. Ace had on a starched white shirt with a red tie, black leather vest, jeans, and red Converse high tops.

Attendees bustled around them as the valet took the keys and gave Merit a parking stub. She looked in her evening bag to make sure she had the opera tickets before she and Ace went up the stairs to the City Terrace overlooking downtown Austin beyond Lady Bird Lake. The view appeared as if a photograph and Merit wished she had her Nikon. She made do by taking a phone selfie of the two of them with downtown Austin as the backdrop.

"Isn't that where Liam Nolan was killed?" Ace said and pointed to a spot along the water's edge.

"Yes," Merit said.

"How is the trial going for Davey?" Ace asked.

"Trial prep is going better," Merit said.

"Good," Ace said.

"Let's not worry about him for one night," Merit smiled and gave him a wink.

"I haven't been to the Opera since last year. It's not Punk like the Butthole Surfers, but everyone needs a little culture now and then," Ace laughed. "I read tonight's soprano graduated from the Butler Opera Center at UT."

"I saw that. Glad you could come home for the weekend, Peaches," Merit said.

"Thanks, Mom, same here," Ace said. "I miss Austin, too."

"It misses you," Merit said.

Ace smiled.

"Every time the trash valet comes to the door, Pepper sits, watches, and wags her tail as if you will walk in at any moment," Merit said.

"I wish I could take her to school with me," Ace said.

"Spring break is coming up. Maybe Port Aransas for a nice vacation for all three of us?" Merit asked.

"I've been meaning to talk to you about that, Mom," Ace said. "There's a school ski trip planned for spring break and I'd like to go."

"Oh. Where is it and who's taking the group?" Merit asked.

"Colorado. Vail. Mr. Jackson will go with us and we'll each have an assigned roommate and ski buddy. No one will be alone at any time. There are also walkie talkies for everyone so he can check on us," Ace said.

He looked hopefully at Merit and smiled.

"Let me check with the school. Send me an email with all the details and phone numbers when you get back next week," Merit said.

"I will," Ace said.

Merit turned toward the door to hide her disappointment. *Growing up so fast*, she thought.

They entered the foyer outside the auditorium and got in line at one of the many bars. Merit ordered a glass of Malbec and Ace had a Dr. Pepper.

♪

Mayor Taylor caught her eye, pretended he didn't see her, and turned into a crowd going onto the balcony level. He was with the family of Barbara Smith Conrad, the famous UT opera singer who had recently passed away.

"What a weenie," Ace said. "You should have hit him harder in that boxing match."

"I wish I had knocked him out," Merit said.

♪

During intermission, Ace ran to the men's room and Merit got another glass of Malbec and stretched her legs by walking around the City Terrace during the cool night air.

Won't be long until summer hits again, she thought.

As she made a second lap, Bo Harding approached her from behind and tapped her on the shoulder.

"Ah," Merit started and turned around causing her skirt to swirl.

He is truly a magnificent looking man, she thought.

"Sorry. Didn't mean to scare you," Bo said. "You look amazing."

"Hi, Bo," Merit said. "I was lost in thought. How are you?"

"I brought you a glass of wine. Red, right?" Bo said and handed her a glass.

Merit's armpits prickled.

"Uh. Thank you. I already have one," Merit said.

"You're almost finished, let's pour this one in here," Bo said.

"No! Uh. Sorry, I just don't like to mix the varietals. Kind of a wine snob," Merit said. She looked at the glass he had handed her and sipped from her own glass.

Ace found his way over to them.

"Ace, you remember Bo Harding, don't you?" Merit asked.

"Yes, Ma'am." Ace said and shook hands with Bo. "Nice to see you again Mr. Harding."

"It's Bo. How are you, Ace?"

"Good, glad to be home for the weekend," Ace said.

"Oh yeah, where do you go to school?" Harding asked.

"Houston. I go to a special school for dyslexic students," Ace said.

"Is that right? We have a show in Houston next month. I'll get you some tickets. Where's the school?" Harding said.

"Wow, thanks. It's..." Ace started.

"That's very nice of you. Please send them to my office," Merit interrupted. "I send a weekly care package down to Houston for him."

"Okay. Ace, what type of music do you like besides opera?" Bo asked.

"I listen to BPM on satellite a lot. It helps me study," Ace said.

"Electronic dance music?" Bo asked.

"Yep. There's a group here in Austin called Wabi Sabi that brings in DJ's from around the world. I've seen one show, but Mom won't let me go to the ones where alcohol is served," Ace said.

"Duh. It's against the law," Merit said.

Ace and Bo laughed.

"I saw your show once at Gruene Hall," Ace said. "Mom took me."

"Really?" Bo looked at Merit with a funny expression on his face.

"You like opera?" Ace asked.

"I like all music. Did you know that Austin hired an acoustician to design the Long Center?" Bo asked.

"I know they channeled the air conditioning through the floor vents to eliminate dead zones," Ace said.

"Right, and the concrete roof and acoustic banners along the walls create a custom-crafted orchestra shell that protects the audience chamber from ambient noises like coughing and candy wrappers," Harding said.

"Yeah, and from outside noises like traffic and thunder," Ace said.

Merit watched with pride as her dyslexic son showed his love of music and art.

"Many artists change their set list when they perform here because of the high-quality acoustics," Harding said.

"I've heard that," Ace said. "Liam Nolan told me."

"I was just about to ask your mother if she's sorted through Liam's songs yet. I know there's one for me in there somewhere," Harding said.

"It's still a bit early. The court hasn't approved the plan for managing the estate. Should be a few more months," Merit said.

A man in a tuxedo snapped a picture of Merit, Ace and Bo. Merit cringed.

"Happens all the time," Bo said.

The lights blinked signaling the end of intermission and Bo stuck out his hand.

"Well, good to see you Merit, Ace," Bo said.

"You, too," Merit said and juggled the two wine glasses to shake his hand."

After Harding walked away, Merit handed the full glass to Ace.

"Peaches, find a place to dump this out, will you? I don't trust any guy bringing me an uninvited glass of wine. Let this be a lesson. If you don't see it come out of the bottle or know the person offering, just get your own drink," Merit said.

Ace looked puzzled.

"Are you being paranoid?" Ace asked.

"If I am, I have good reason to be. Just trust your Mom on this one," Merit said.

41

Merit sat in the back of Travis County Criminal Courtroom Number Three and watched Kim Wan and Jason Ellsworth, the assistant D.A., select a jury. Voir dire took almost seven hours as the panelists were vetted and accepted or removed one by one. Kim Wan moved expertly through his questions to the panel and walked near Davey often touching his shoulder or giving him an encouraging nod. Kim Wan's attempts to influence the jury had already begun, Merit noticed. He was making Davey seem vulnerable, likable, and innocent.

"We have a jury," Judge Crow said from his high perch. "Ladies and gentlemen we will shortly break for the day. On Monday, you will begin to hear evidence regarding the murder of Liam Ray Nolan. The prosecutor and the defense will both have an opportunity to lay out their cases and you must listen to all of the evidence before coming to a verdict."

Several of the jurors nodded at the judge.

Davey pleaded with his eyes.

"Over the weekend, you must refrain from reading the newspapers and any online materials about the evidence in this trial. I admonish you to give this young man your best effort and devote your full attention to the evidence as presented here and here alone. The prosecution is seeking the death penalty and you owe this court

187

and the community an honest and untainted verdict," Judge Crow said.

♪

Merit waited for Kim Wan outside the courtroom and walked him back to his office down the street. It was already dark outside and the cool night air and sweet smell of the trees reminded Merit of why she lived in Austin.

A car drove by with an old Jerry Jeff Walker tune, *Up Against the Wall*, playing through the open windows.

"I can't hear that song without singing Redneck Mother," Merit said.

"Me too," Kim Wan said.

"Is it as bad as it looks for Davey?" Merit asked.

"It's pretty bad," Kim Wan said. "The totality of the evidence is overwhelming."

"But, it's all circumstantial. Even the photos don't show him actually killing Liam," Merit said.

"True, but that's what circumstantial means. You know that. When so much evidence points to what probably happened, that skepticism tips over into belief," Kim Wan said.

"What can I do to help you?" Merit asked.

"I'll let you know if I think of something. For now, a prayer would be good," Kim Wan said.

42

L.A. and HackerDude Skyped from their respective work places. "Davey Bell was indicted based in part on drone photos showing his presence near Liam. I want to get all the drone pics I can from the night of the murder. I need to know what's out there. Is there a registration of some sort for drones?" L.A. asked.

"The licensing is from the federal government because the FAA controls air space. Flight plans are supposed to be filed, but not everyone complies. Each state has different regs. Most drones operate in the gray space between all the confusing rules and regulations," HackerDude said.

"How do you know you can get the photos then?" L.A. asked.

"Hobbyists originated drone technology, not the military. I can get them because all the signals that go up to the cloud show which drone was used on what day and where. Once I pinpoint the date, we'll have all the info we want. The cloud is so easy to hack."

"Nothing is private anymore," L.A. said.

"Right," HackerDude said. "I can have it within a few hours."

"That's fast. Can you safely send them to my computer?" L.A. asked.

"Yep. This area of the law is so new, I doubt we'd even be prosecuted if we were caught."

"Well, let's don't be the test case. Cover your tracks," L.A. said.

"Always."

L.A. sat with his feet on his desk and thought about Merit as he looked out the window. He would win. He would get all he wanted. He was close. He could feel it.

He was worried about the drone pictures. What if they showed something he didn't want seen? What if they cleared Davey? How would he control the estate then? The gin in his drink warmed him and he reminisced about all the regrets of his life. The memories would not leave him alone. The pressure started to build inside as he thought of Dahl.

He paced the room but did not stop at the bar. He looked at the closet door and resisted going inside. He went back to his desk and looked at his email. Nothing yet from HackerDude.

He remembered being bullied in grade school. He couldn't push the memories of being called Shrimp, Tiny Dick, Shorty, and all the other rotten names his schoolmates had chosen for him. He also remembered how Dahl had defended him. Beautiful Dahl.

L.A. fidgeted with some paperwork and tried to keep the swelling urge at bay. Finally, he gave up and went into the dark closet.

He bolted the door, sat on the lonely stool and rocked back and forth slowly, then with increased vigor. He chanted his usual mantra about Dahl.

"I'm so sorry. I didn't mean it. I'm so sorry. I'm so sorry."

The mantra and subsequent scream placed him in an out of body experience that led to subsequent release. After the discharge of tension, he rocked less violently then finally settled into a gentle sway. L.A. stayed in that state for a long time until his eyes opened and he looked around to see where he was. As his rage and terror subsided, he became calm and purposeful.

He clenched his fists and stood up with fresh energy and vengeance flowing through his veins.

43

Merit woke up late on Saturday to the doorbell ringing. Ace's Cairn Terrier, Pepper, barked at the door. Merit jerked to attention in the middle of a dream that faded quickly, but remained frightening.

She looked at her phone and saw a text from the desk downstairs that her grocery delivery was coming up. She had forgotten that she'd placed the online order the night before with Whole Foods. She remembered, from her law school days, the original Whole Foods just a few blocks from the new anchor store. She had helped them clean out the mud when it flooded during her third year. One more thing she missed about old small-town Austin.

She flung on a white robe, went to the living room, and looked out the peephole into the hallway. Either the delivery woman was legit or she had spent a lot of money on groceries to cover her entry. Merit let her in.

"Sorry it took so long for me to answer. Slept in today," Merit said.

"No problem," she said as she set the groceries inside the doorway.

"Thanks," Merit said.

"Have a nice day," the delivery woman said and left.

After Merit stowed the groceries in fridge and pantry and gave Pepper a treat, she took her tea and a gluten free blueberry muffin onto the balcony of her high-rise condo. She'd been rotating her grains after reading online articles about wheat contamination.

What's the use of trying to be healthy when your world is falling apart? I can't even answer the door without jumping out of my skin, she thought.

She sat at a glass table and opened her laptop to Austin9Online. Pepper made a circle then sat on her foot. While the site came up, she looked over downtown Austin. This was her home, her favorite place in the world, her neighborhood and front yard. Someone was systematically taking it from her one step at a time and all attempts to stop them to date had failed her.

She hoped that the new security measures Ag and Tech Security had put into place would cease the spying on her office machines, but she could not control the fake news that seemed to be multiplying with the reproductive capability of rabbits.

The websites had reported increasing sightings of her with various young men and had photo-shopped pictures to prove the encounters. Several sites had carried the fake news of malfeasance against her clients.

She scrolled through the news articles praying silently that she would not be in the news today.

No luck.

Bridges Accused of Embezzlement from Local Charity.

Merit clicked on the article and read the full text.

Local attorney Merit Bridges is being investigated surrounding allegations of embezzlement and personal use of funds from Texas KnockOut Illiteracy. Bridges, known as a top fundraiser for the non-profit, has been spotlighted by several online news organizations as having used charity funds for personal use and allocating funds inappropriately to undeserving recipients.

The Austin D.A.'s office has put together a team to investigate the allegations and determine the origin of evidentiary documents released by several watchdog websites. The letters and bank statements posted by the sites are convincing evidence of Bridges' guilt in the theft and the use of non-profit funds for personal purposes such as travel, luxury items, and personal entertainment benefiting her law firm.

The State Bar of Texas is considering disbarment proceedings against Bridges. The bar expects to conclude its investigation by early next week.

Merit stopped reading. Tears puddled in her eyes and spilled over as she looked at the dome of the State Capitol and the sun shining on the Austin skyline. The city looked surreal in light of current events. She could not connect to her home. It's as if the city was evaporating before her.

She shivered in the breeze, then started to shake. No matter what she did from this moment on, she would never again be seen as Austin's golden girl punching out the mayor in a fun boxing match. She'd never see someone whispering without wondering if it was about her. She'd never walk the city streets without second guessing the thoughts of every person she passed.

The next day, Merit sat at her desk typing on her keyboard. Betty stood beside her with her hand on Merit's shoulder.

"I'm finished," Merit said and pointed at the screen. "Take a look."

Betty read out loud:

Dear Board of Directors, Knock Out Literacy:

I'm writing to you today with a heavy heart. As you all know, I have been accused of embezzling money from our organization for personal gain. I've also been accused of using non-profit funds for personal benefit. While I vehemently deny these allegations, I cannot ignore the publicity surrounding them nor the negative impact it is having on Knock Out Literacy, the board, and our ability to raise funds.

*Therefore, it is with deep regret and sadness that I submit this
resignation to the board of directors effective immediately.*

Very truly yours,

Merit Bridges

Betty pulled a tissue from her sleeve and wiped a tear from her
eye.

"Oh, Darlin', I'm so sorry," Betty said. "You built this
organization almost single handedly."

Merit had worked for years on the festival, making it a go-
to event alongside Austin City Limits Music Festival, SXSW, and
Willie Nelson's Fourth of July Picnic.

Merit turned her head into Betty's side and muffled her sobs
in Betty's dress.

Betty stroked Merit's ponytail and twirled it between her
fingers until the crying ceased.

"Everything will turn out alright," Betty said. "It hurts now,
but out of suffering always comes resurrection."

"I don't believe it. What have I done to deserve this?" Merit
said.

"You don't deserve it," Betty said. "This too shall pass."

"I don't like airing my dirty laundry," Merit said.

"Why is it dirty laundry?" Betty asked. "Are you doing
something dirty?"

"No, but others may see it that way," Merit said.

"And what if they do." Betty said. "Anyone who doesn't like
what you do can go butt a rubber stump," Betty said. "You'll come
to terms with this in your own private way."

Ag entered the APD downtown office and checked his gun before
going through security. He waved at Chaplain who was standing at
the coffee pot near his office door.

"Want a cup?" Chaplain said.

"Sure," Ag said and took a paper cup off the stack.

"Come on in. What brings you by today?" Chaplain asked as he moved behind his desk and sat down.

Ag slouched in a chair before the desk and stretched his long torso and legs out before him.

"That cyberstalking problem has gotten worse," Ag said.

"How so?"

"Fake news is trending all over the internet and local blogs have picked it up as gospel. It's damaging Merit's reputation and harming her business. They've crossed over from mischief into illegal activity, possibly for profit," Ag said. "Is there such a crime as theft of someone's livelihood through fake news?"

"Give me an update," Chaplain said.

"Well, since we last met the online fake news has more than doubled. Documents, purportedly from the mayor's office, have been posted along with video and photo-shopped pictures. The pics put Merit in places she's never been doing things she's not done." Ag said.

"Good grief," Chaplain said.

"Worse thing, she's had to resign from the charity that she built from the ground up. She formed it for Ace and others like him. She will protect it even if it means she has to leave it. It means that much to her," Ag said.

"I'll put some more eyes on it, but you know this is like chasing a phantom," Chaplain said.

"Anything you can do. We've got some tech guys on it too, but we need all the help we can get. She has more clients leaving the firm," Ag said.

"I understand. I'll see what we can do," Chaplain said.

"Anything new on Liam Nolan's murder?" Ag asked.

"We've got someone in jail for that," Chaplain said.

"He's out on bail. Living with his dead daddy's NA sponsor. No one believes this kid is guilty but your prosecutor," Ag said.

"Why is it every time you walk in here I have more work to do?" Chaplain asked.

"Glad to help," Ag said, but he didn't laugh at his own joke.

44

L.A. arrived at the Travis County Probate Court with his attorney, Thomas Tipton. Both wore suits costing in excess of five thousand dollars and shoes with buttery leather uppers and hard leather soles. Their briefcases matched their leather shoes, and L.A.'s had his initials in gold just below the handles.

They took their seats at the plaintiff's table and unpacked files, laptops, and MontBlanc pens, red for Tipton and black for L.A. The courtroom was empty as they had arrived early to prepare.

"Remember, you'll be sitting right here when you're speaking to the judge," Herman said.

"I know," L.A. said.

"Look at me when I ask, then turn to the judge to answer," Tipton said. "When Bridges cross-examines you, look at the judge the entire time."

"Right. Got it," L.A. said.

Merit and Val sat in their stylish but understated courtroom attire. L.A. looked over at Merit and smirked. She turned her head toward Val and pretended not to notice.

What an ass, she thought. Val's returned look mirrored her thinking.

After the initial courtroom rituals, Judge Herman got down to business.

"This is a hearing on the matter of the Executor of the Estate of Liam Raymond Nolan," she said. "Please proceed, Mr. Tipton."

"The petitioner, Mr. L.A. Baron, requests that Ms. Bridges be removed as Executrix and that he be substituted as Executor in her stead. Ms. Bridges is currently under investigation for embezzlement from Texas KnockOut Illiteracy. She is in a position of trust for that charity just as she is in the probate which is presently before this court. She has been accused of betraying that trust and should be held suspect until the matter is cleared," Mr. Tipton said. "My client Mr. Baron is uniquely positioned to serve as substitute Executor as he is currently managing part of the portfolio of Mr. Nolan under a contract with him, has extensive experience in the music community, and an unsullied reputation for honesty and fairness in his business dealings."

"Anything further before we hear from Ms. Bridges?" Judge Herman said.

"Yes, Your Honor, my client has been managing a portion of Liam Nolan's catalogue of music for many years. He has intricate knowledge of the music business that no amount of research by Ms. Bridges will replace," Mr. Tipton said.

Merit was on her feet. "Your Honor."

"Ok, Ms. Bridges. Settle down. You'll get your turn. I'll hear from Mr. Baron first. Swear him in," Judge Herman said.

After L.A. was sworn and settled in the witness box, his attorney began a line of questioning that left Merit and Val steaming and baffled.

"Mr. Baron," Mr. Tipton said. "Please explain to the court what you have done in an attempt to work in harmony with Ms. Bridges."

"I have attempted to set several meetings with her, and to provide my expertise," L.A. said.

"In what way?" Mr. Tipton asked.

"For example, with regard to the accounting she's reviewing, which is very detailed and specific to the music industry," L.A. said.

"The nerve," Merit whispered to Val behind her hand.

"What else?" Mr. Tipton asked.

"I have also attempted to give her a calendar of upcoming release dates for various music which might support the increase of income to the estate by association and proper marketing," L.A. said.

Merit looked at Val and shook her head.

What a bunch of smoke and mirrors, Merit thought.

Mr. Tipton returned to the petitioner's table and retrieved a file. He dropped two pages in front of Merit and took a duplicate of those two pages to the judge.

"As you can see from this correspondence, Your Honor, Ms. Bridges is out of control and unprofessional in her interaction with Mr. Baron," Tipton said.

"Objection, Your Honor," Merit said. "There's no proof of the origin of these emails. I barely know Mr. Baron."

"Hold on a second, Ms. Bridges. Let's get all this on the record," Judge Herman said.

"Mr. Baron," Mr. Tipton said. "Why do you think you should be Executor of Liam Nolan's estate?"

"I am not thin skinned. I can take a hit in the business now and then, but Ms. Bridges is being investigated for embezzlement of funds from Texas KnockOut Illiteracy. The organization has accepted her resignation, which I believe was forced upon her," L.A. said.

"What does that have to do with Liam Nolan's estate?" Mr. Tipton asked.

"Ms. Bridges is associated with Davey Ray Nolan who is accused of killing Liam Nolan. She is in a position to embezzle from the estate, as she embezzled from Texas KnockOut Illiteracy, and has very little supervision," L.A. said.

"Objection. Davey Nolan still is entitled to the presumption of innocence, and this court has oversight regarding all purchases and payments of the estate which I might make," Merit said.

"You'll get your turn, Ms. Bridges," Judge Herman said then turned to L.A. "Sustained. Mr. Baron, limit your testimony to your personal knowledge."

"Sorry, Your Honor," L.A. said.

"Let me rephrase," Mr. Tipton said. "Mr. Baron, what leads you to believe that you would be a better executor for the estate of Liam Nolan?" Tipton asked.

"I'm bonded. I have a history of handling musician's funds in the millions of dollars. I have never been accused of taking one red cent from anyone I've managed," L.A. said. "Further, I've won every music award that a manager and producer can garner."

"Couldn't anyone who is trustworthy do the job you are asking to do? What makes you particularly suitable to take over the estate management?" Tipton asked.

"I already have a portion of the estate's funds coming through my office trust account in the form of royalties paid by both domestic and foreign music distributors for rights on several songs, including *Fever Stomp*. I actually sold the rights to *Fever Stomp* to TofuGrind, a Japanese company. The song is now the most profitable title in Liam Nolan's Japanese portfolio. I am the only person who is uniquely qualified to perform this service."

"Where are most of the funds from Liam Nolan's estate to be paid?" Tipton asked.

"They are slated to be paid into non-profits very similar to the one Ms. Bridges is accused of looting."

Merit stood and shouted. "Objection! There are no recipients established at this point."

The judge started to respond.

"Withdrawn. Thank you, Mr. Baron. No further questions, Your Honor," Tipton said.

L.A. left the witness box, shot his cuffs, and strutted to his seat like a banty rooster.

When Merit got her turn, she was sworn in and sat in the witness box. Since she was both attorney and witness at this point, she enumerated all the reasons she should be in charge of the estate. Merit did her best to convince the Judge to delay his decision to remove her as Executrix, but it fell on deaf ears.

"Ms. Bridges," Judge Herman said. "It may be that you have been falsely accused, and it may also be that you can clear your name and re-present to the court, but I must err on the side of caution at this juncture and remove you as executrix."

"But, Your Honor," Merit said.

"As there are no living heirs other than Mr. Nolan's son, or other parties appearing to be interested in the estate, I appoint Mr. L.A. Baron as substitute executor, effective immediately."

L.A. and Tipton gave a visual high five, packed up, and left Merit and Val sitting in stunned silence.

45

Davey sat in the TV room of the shelter with about a dozen other men. No one was smiling. It was a depressing environment and although posters with encouraging slogans hung on the walls and Reverend Hightower tried to lift them up every chance he got, there was no denying that short of being on the street, this was as low as life gets. Maybe worse than the street. At least out there, some measure of freedom was felt and the constant foraging for food and shelter made for a busy day with small victories from time to time. Here, in the shelter, nothing moved. Everything and everyone was stagnant as if life occurred all around the world except here.

Davey waited his turn then checked his email on the community computer. A sign by the desk said "FIVE MINUTE LIMIT". He opened his Gmail account and found a note from what appeared to be the Law Office of Merit Bridges. It said: "Kim Wan has bad news. Get over to his office ASAP."

Davey relinquished the computer and paced the room. His anxiety showed with each jerky movement. He finally plopped down on one of the worn sofas and folded his arms across his chest.

Ash, in his customary veteran patches and camouflage got a paper cup of water. His disguise had worked like a charm since he originally infiltrated the shelter with L.A. and started the dance of manipulation with Hightower. Ash watched Davey over the edge of the cup as he pretended to drink. He waited for the right moment, then sat down beside Davey.

"How's it going, man," Ash said.

"It's not. I need to see my lawyer and I can't get a ride over to the office," Davey said.

"It's the weekend," Ash said.

"He's working. We're in trial," Davey said.

"There's a bus," Ash said.

"No money," Davey said.

"I don't have any either or I'd lend you a few bucks. You could walk," Ash said.

"It's over ten miles. They'd be closed by the time I got there," Davey said.

"You could borrow Reverend Hightower's car," Ash said. "He just got a new one given to the shelter by some rich donor."

"Yeah, right," Davey said.

"No, really. He's let other men borrow it for good reasons. It's for the use of the shelter. You could ask him," Ash said.

"You think?" Davey asked.

"Sure. I just saw him go into his office," Ash said.

Davey stepped down the hallway and looked into Reverend Hightower's open door. Ash came up behind him but did not join in.

"Hi Reverend. I need to get to an appointment at my lawyer's office and I need a ride or some money for the bus. Ash said you sometimes lend your car out. Could I borrow it or do you have any petty cash? Is it even okay to ask?" Davey asked.

Reverend Hightower looked past Davey at Ash. He took a deep breath and sat for a moment. He seemed to come to a decision. He took the keys from his pocket and handed them to Davey.

"Okay, sure," Reverend Hightower said. "It's the new brown Chrysler parked in the first spot out the back door."

"Thanks. What time should I have it back?" Davey asked.

"Doesn't matter," Reverend Hightower said. He averted his eyes.

♪

Davey drove down Interstate 35 on the feeder road, passed Sixth Street, and followed the arrow on a temporary traffic sign to move over into the left lane. The air conditioner kicked up to full blast and he tried to turn it off without taking his eyes off the road. Just as he gave up pushing buttons, it turned off on its own.

His ankle bracelet he'd been ordered to wear by the court began to vibrate on his leg and make a slight buzzing sound. *Did I cross some invisible barrier?* The vibration stopped and he continued on.

All of the streets into downtown were blocked with orange and white striped sawhorses. Thousands of people milled around the traffic barricades and orange cones, enjoying the spring weather and yearly South By Southwest Music Festival. Tunes floated through the air and mixed into a strange blend of hip hop, blues and country. Davey tried to remember how to get around downtown on the east side and back over to Kim Wan's office on the west.

The radio suddenly blared and Davey's attempts to turn it down or off were useless. The windshield wipers swung back and forth in macabre rhythm to the music then stopped.

"What the hell? Crazy car. No wonder they gave it to the shelter," Davey said.

The engine slowed down and the car began to crawl down the street. Davey pressed the gas, but there was no response. The steering became very stiff. Then, it froze and he could not steer at all.

The car turned left on its own onto Ninth Street and broke down the barrier.

"Oh no, this is a one way!" Davey said.

He could not turn the wheel. The steering wheel turned on its own even when he tried to hold it. Davey's ankle bracelet began to buzz again and the stinging increased. The windshield wipers and radio came back on. Everything was going haywire at once.

The car turned right onto Red River and accelerated. People were everywhere. A policeman jumped out of the way near the barricade. He could not turn the car off Red River. It was the longest block of Davey's life.

Not only was the car out of control, another event started to increase Davey's terror. The ankle bracelet began to burn his skin through his sock. He tried to pull the bracelet from his skin and burned his fingers. He fanned his jeans over his ankle and his pants leg caught on fire. The stinging and heat were unbearable. He began to scream. He tried to open the door, but it was locked. He removed his safety belt and leaned across the console and swatted the fire from his pant leg. He reared up and pushed both feet against the window but it did not break.

The car hit several food carts as people jumped out of the way on both sides. A block later, he approached Tenth Street and hit a couple. The woman was thrown fifteen feet onto the sidewalk. The vehicle picked up speed and approached Eleventh Street. Davey's car hit a taxi cab and a motorcycle rider crossing the street. The woman on the back of the bike was crushed.

Upon hearing the commotion, several policemen began to run after the car and several more into the fray from the side streets. The car bounced up onto the sidewalk where it hit two more pedestrians. Three policemen stood in front of the car, took aim and fired seventeen bullets into the windshield and Davey. They jumped from the car's path just in time to avoid impact.

The car veered into a parked food truck and finally came to a stop.

♪

Red Thallon stood on the site of the horrific events from the last day of SXSW. She positioned herself in front of the food truck where the final stop occurred and held the microphone in her hand.

"Davey Ray Nolan, also known as Davey Ray Bell committed suicide by cop according to the official spokesperson from APD. Davey Nolan ended his life after careening down this section of Red River, killing five pedestrians, and seriously injuring twenty-three more. One Austin policeman is in critical condition at Brackenridge Hospital and many families are arranging funerals for their loved ones," Red said.

She half turned her body to look back at the scene behind yellow police tape then turned back toward the camera.

"Davey Nolan was out on bail during the trial of his life for allegedly killing his father, Liam Nolan, one of Austin's own and best known for his hit song *Fever Stomp*."

The cameraman zoomed in on Red's perfectly made up face.

"Davey Nolan was facing the death penalty if convicted. He purportedly stole the car he was driving from Reverend Morton Hightower at the shelter where he was staying while out on bail. Hightower was not available for comment at the time of this broadcast, but his written statement confirmed that the car was stolen from the parking lot at the St. John's Men's Shelter. Several other men at the shelter confirmed that Davey Nolan was despondent and anxious before he left the shelter and took the car."

"Local attorneys Merit Bridges and Kim Wan Thibodeaux refused to be part of this interview, however both said that there had been a recent turn in the case giving Davey Nolan hope in the trial. Just what that event was is still covered under the attorney client privilege, but what we do know is that it wasn't enough to deter this young man from taking out as many people as he could on the way to ending his own life."

46

Davey's funeral was held at the same place as Liam's per Davey's request in his short will that Merit had drafted on pancake day.

Only Merit, Betty, Kim Wan, Reverend Hightower, and a few men from the shelter were present. Louellen and her body guard boyfriend arrived at the last minute and Merit started the service.

"We were all very fond of Davey," Merit said. She began to tear up and could not speak. Betty was crying softly into a handkerchief she had pulled from her sleeve.

Reverend Hightower walked up beside Merit and took over the service. He went on so long about the scriptures that everyone stopped crying and just became bored. He finally wrapped up the service with a prayer.

Merit poured Davey's ashes into the lake and that was that. It was more like a surreal movie than a funeral. Merit wasn't sure if she spoke the language or needed an interpreter.

"Let's get a drink," Betty said to Merit after saying goodbye to Kim Wan.

"Let's slip away. I have no intention of joining into anything else today," Merit said.

Merit held Betty's arm to steady her on the cracked sidewalk. When she looked up, Louellen was standing in front of them.

"You killed my boy," Louellen said. "You're responsible for what happened to my Davey."

"Your Davey," Betty said.

"Hold it," Merit said. "Let's keep moving."

"Don't think you'll get away with this," Louellen yelled after them.

"Now she wants to be a mother," Merit said.

"I know what kind of mother you mean," Betty said.

♪

Merit and Betty sat at the Driskill Hotel Bar in chairs covered with cowhide under huge longhorns mounted on the wall. They sat as far away from the piano as they could so they could talk. A tall lanky woman covered a vintage Marcia Ball tune.

"Drink your wine, Darlin'. I know it's so sad about Davey, but you need your strength," Betty said.

"Why? Why do I need strength? I don't understand how this could happen," Merit said.

"You're not buying into Louellen's bullshit are you?" Betty asked and took a long pull on her whiskey. "That woman is crazier than all git out."

"No, it's not about her. It's me. I don't see what good it serves anyone for a sweet boy like Davey to die," Merit said. "That kid never hurt a soul. He just wanted a father," Merit said.

"We all die. It's just a matter of when," Betty said.

"Davey's death reminds me of Tony. It just brings it all back," Merit said.

"Tony was sick, that's different," Betty said.

"My husband is gone. Loss is loss," Merit said.

"Yes, but you know the difference. Drink your wine," Betty said.

"Over half my clients have left," Merit said.

"Lack of trust is more about them than about you," Betty said.

Merit picked up the glass and looked at the red liquid.

"Darlin', there's no way to have a hero without the dilemma. We would never rise up if we weren't in strife," Betty said.

"I guess," Merit said.

"Take a few days. Go down to your beach house - walk and read a good book. Restore yourself. There's a fight ahead and in my opinion, you're the winner of the next go 'round," Betty said.

"Hero? I'm ruined in Austin. I'll never be a hero again," Merit said.

"You know you didn't do any of the things reported in the news," Betty said.

"You can't un-ring a bell. No one will see the good news, but they'll always remember the bad," Merit said.

"You'll know," Betty said.

"That doesn't help," Merit said.

"It will. Have a little faith. Lord willing and the creek don't rise, you'll be out of this mess before summer is over," Betty said.

"It'll never be the same," Merit said.

"It never is," Betty said.

47

Merit left Austin on Highway 183 at sunset. The Texas sky was painted coral and purple over a blue backdrop. She tuned in Folksingers on satellite radio and listened to an unplugged cover of Townes Van Zandt's *Pancho and Lefty*. The melancholy melody reflected Merit's mood and her shoulders slumped toward the steering wheel. Pepper put her head on Merit's leg and looked up at her with sad eyes.

Merit clicked the telephone icon on the steering wheel and said, "Call Ace, mobile." She immediately hit the stop icon and chastised herself for her weakness. Ace had gone skiing with his class for spring break in Vail. Why involve him further? She was glad he was having a good time and unaware of the depth of what she was going through.

She stopped at Kreuz BBQ in Lockhart out of habit and filled a small ice chest with brisket and sides. Since Ace wasn't with her, she skipped the sausage and his other traditional road trip favorites.

When the meat carver at Kruez made his usual jokes, she faked a laugh. She felt alone and numb. Even the smoky aroma didn't stimulate her senses.

Maybe I'll be hungry later, she thought.

Merit continued through Rockport to Aransas Pass and took the Charles W. Heald ferry boat over the ship channel to Port Aransas. She and Pepper looked for their little dolphin buddies in the water along the way, but she couldn't see them in the dark. It was one of the few times none came to leap by the ferry to greet her.

Merit drove off the boat and down McAlister then toward her beach house. On the radio, Norah Jones crooned a tune about not knowing why she didn't come. At the house, lights were on and the refrigerator was stocked with the basics thanks to Betty calling down to the housekeeper to make it ready. A nice bottle of Duckhorn Napa Valley Merlot was in the wine rack.

She pulled the cork, poured a glass, sat outside, and listened to the ocean. Once she felt the sound and rhythm of the waves washing over her, she began to cry. She grieved the loss of her reputation, the attitude of her fair-weather friends, her loss of status in the Austin community and her confused sense of self. Who was she if not paired with those who had abandoned her? What was her role if she were to lose all her clients, or worse, be disbarred?

She refilled her glass and tried to see the water. Without the moon out, there was a vast black void where the water should be. Only the sound of the never-ending waves told her the shoreline was out there.

She thought back over the last months since she and the mayor were boxing onstage at the music festival. She thought of poor Liam and Davey and their sad and violent endings.

She thought of the list of clients and enemies she had provided for Chaplain. Each foe had a reason to be angry, but to destroy her reputation and strip her bare took a very vengeful soul. Evil. Someone who would stop at nothing. Could any of her clients or business opponents hate her that much?

She looked back at every event that had hit her from the fake news to cyberbullying to the challenge of her law license.

She saw a ladder of descent in her mind's eye down into a dungeon where Pluto, the god of the underworld waited for her. Each step was labeled with another assault on her reputation and livelihood.

She thought of the good she tried to do by volunteering at the legal clinic. She always felt that karma would keep her safe from all intruders and evil doers. Apparently not this time. All her good deeds seemed to go unnoticed by the gods of balance.

She felt alone, abandoned, bereft, and lost. Against her better judgment, she drank the last of the bottle of wine and went to bed. Her dreams were fitful and held chases by newspaper reporters, empty file folders, and blank pages on her computer screen.

She wept in her sleep.

♪

The next day, Merit woke up with a nagging headache. She took Pepper for a long walk on the beach to clear her brain and sweat out the last of the wine. She beseeched the ocean. The veil didn't lift.

After a shower, she left Pepper in the small side yard and drove the BMW into town. She slowed behind a golf cart barely moving. She pulled into the other lane and looked around, but oncoming traffic prevented her from passing so she jerked the wheel to pull the BMW back in her lane. The cart finally turned into the candy store and she picked up speed.

"Hell," she said. "What's the rush anyway?"

She continued over to the Ellis Memorial Library on Avenue A. There was construction going on at the end of the building.

Even Port A won't stay the same for me, she thought.

She browsed around the mystery section then checked out several books and a couple of DVDs, older movies she'd missed during the last Oscar season. It had been a while since she'd had this much free time on her hands.

Next, she stopped at IGA, the local grocery store, and picked up more wine and a few extra things for the house. She looked through a rack of books and thumbed through a yoga magazine at the checkout line, then put two books and the mag in her basket. She saw several varieties of dark chocolate on another rack and snagged an assortment of that too.

Merit looked into the basket.

Who's buying all this stuff? she thought.

Merit drove onto 361 and headed toward her house. *I'm Drinking Through It* by Jack Ingram came on satellite radio. As Jack sang about all the ways he'd been hurt, Merit made her own list. She turned down to the beach, opened the sunroof and drove along the edge of the waves feeling the second deepest regret of her life. The caw of the seagulls echoed overhead. The only time she remembered being this sad was when her husband had taken his life in the backyard of their home. She had found him slumped over in a lawn chair, gun on the ground.

At that moment, she had known what it was like not only to feel wrong but to be wrong in her core. She must have been less-than for him to leave her that way. She must not have been enough. She could not keep him alive.

The satellite radio began to skip and finally quit all together. Merit tapped the information screen.

As if that would do any good, she thought.

The computer jumped to navigation without her direction.

"Strange," she said.

The indicator at the bottom of the map screen showed an incoming call from Ag. She hit the telephone button on the steering wheel to accept the call.

"Merit, it's Ag. How are you?"

"Okay, I guess. I don't know really," Merit said.

"I hate to add to your burden, but I've got some bad news," Ag said.

"What now?" Merit asked.

Merit felt the steering wheel jerk. She grabbed the wheel tighter and looked in her rearview mirror to see if she'd hit a hole in the sand or a log left from a bonfire. Nothing.

"Davey did not commit suicide," Ag said. "He was murdered. Chaplain got the report on the car this morning."

"What? How?" Merit asked.

She tried to focus on what Ag was saying and determine what was going on with the BMW at the same time.

"The car he was driving was taken over by a hacker and Davey could not control the vehicle. Witnesses saw him trying to kick out the glass. Now we know why," Ag said.

The steering wheel jerked again and it felt to Merit as though the power steering was failing.

"What the hell?" Merit asked.

"Davey. He wasn't responsible for hurting those people," Ag said.

"No, I heard you. It's my car. It's going crazy," Merit said.

"What? Can you stop the car?" Ag asked.

Merit pumped the brakes to no effect. Her speed increased. Ahead was a family of beach goers. She could not avoid them. The steering wheel jerked from her hands. She tried to put the car into park but the gear would not budge. The group ahead screamed and dispersed as she plowed through their shade tent and ran over a folding chair. She pushed the start button to try to kill the engine, but it didn't respond.

"Ag, I can't stop the car," Merit said.

"Merit, get out of there. Oh, my god," Ag said. "Merit... Merit!"

Merit saw a large silver motor home parked on the right and the water on the left. She was headed straight for the back of the giant mobile monster. She jerked her seatbelt tightly across her chest and held onto the wheel as tightly as she could. The BMW plowed into a pile of sand which spun her to the right. She hit the side of the motor home with a glancing blow which caused her SUV to bank like a pool ball and flip. The Beemer turned over and over rolling toward the water like a giant beach ball.

A young mother snatched her toddler out of the way just before the BMW hit their sandcastle. Plastic buckets and shovels went flying. The SUV bounced into the air, flipped once more, and landed on its side in the water. The interior started to fill.

Merit lay still with her eyes closed.

"Merit!" Ag yelled on the phone.

The phone went dead.

Merit woke up seconds later to the echo of Ag's voice as the water rose and climbed to her shoulder. She bent her head to the side to breath. She pushed on the door above her but it wouldn't open. She tried to climb out, but the seatbelt had her trapped. She searched around her hip for the button and released it as the water crept up her face. Her eyes and nose filled with stinging salt water. Four tan arms reached into the sunroof and pulled her through the opening as she lost consciousness.

♪

Merit lay under a blanket on a stretcher in the back of an ambulance with oxygen flowing into her nose from a transparent tube. She felt a strange sensation of being larger than herself, larger than the ocean, larger than the entire world. The feeling was energizing and indisputable. She was saved because she had things to do in the world. She had been snatched from a watery death to continue to live a life worth living. She awoke slowly to the real world and could hear the seagulls overhead. She felt the presence of another person nearby. She finally sat up and watched the melee around her.

"Take it easy," the paramedic said.

"Thanks. I'm okay," Merit said, but she didn't try to stand. She remembered the BMW and the beach and the rising water.

"How did I get out of the SUV?"

"Two good Samaritans swam out and pulled you through the sunroof. You were very lucky," he said.

"I'd like to thank them," Merit said.

"The Port A police have their statements. You can run by the police station and get all that information when you're up to it."

"Do you have a phone I can borrow?" Merit asked.

Merit called Ag from the ambulance as she watched the wrecker pull her BMW onto the beach. Water poured from the windows and wheel wells in a gush with seaweed and shells floating in the discharge. Another BMW gone.

Several beachgoers walked up to watch the spectacle.

"You don't see that every day," a man said to his wife.

"Not in sleepy Port Aransas," she replied.

Merit blinked and focused her eyes and tried to remember Ag's number. She was so accustomed to speed dial and so discombobulated she could not get past the 512 area code. She thought for a moment, then called Betty. That's a number she'd had burned into her memory for eons.

"Betty, it's me. Don't get upset. I had an accident, sort of. I'm fine. I just need you to patch in Ag and I'll tell you all about what's happened. I can't remember his number," Merit said.

"Hang on, Darlin'," Betty said.

When Ag joined the conversation, Merit told Betty in brief what had happened and asked Ag to fill in the rest later.

"What do you need right now?" Ag asked.

"I have to give this phone back, so I need to be quick. I wanted to let you know I'm okay," Merit said.

"Thank goodness," Ag said.

"I need a car. I also want you to know we must do something. No more playing by the rules. I'll be back in Austin tomorrow, and we're going to find out who's behind this and go after them," Merit said.

"Darlin', you don't sound like yourself," Betty said. "Are you sure you're all right?"

"I haven't been this all right in a long time," Merit said.

"What can we do to help?" Betty asked.

"Ag, please send your man to Houston to watch over Ace, just as a precaution."

"You got it," Ag said.

"I'll need a rental," Merit said.

"I'll get a car delivered to you from Corpus Christi as soon as possible." Betty said. "Can you get back to your beach house?"

"I can. The ambulance will give me a ride," Merit said.

"Ambulance? Try to stay calm," Betty said to Merit and to herself.

"I am calm. I haven't felt this calm in months. No more. I mean it. I've had enough." Merit said.

48

Merit returned to Austin and had a physical by her western doctor and by her chiropractor at Betty's insistence. When she was released, Ag took her home where Betty had a big pot of her famous *Feel Better Soup* waiting. It was full of safety, security, love and a bunch of vegetables.

"Just what the doctor ordered," Merit said. "Thank you."

The next day, Merit rallied the office staff to go through the entire list of suspected clients again. Betty and Val sat in the guest chairs in Merit's office. They split up the list they had provided to Chaplain.

"Val, you take A to L and Betty, you take M to Z. I'm going to look at all of them. We have to figure out who's doing this and why," Merit said.

A few blocks away in his office, L.A. listened through his earpiece to the conversation in Merit's office. When she gave her staff their marching orders, he laughed.

"You have no clue," L.A. said.

49

L.A. took a plain sheet of paper and writing with his right hand, although he was left handed, penned a legal document.

> *I, Liam Raymond Nolan, being of sound mind and body do hereby declare this my Last Will and Testament. It is written entirely in my own hand and contains all of my wishes regarding my estate. I revoke all prior wills and codicils executed by me and leave the entirety of my estate in trust for charities to be named and administered by my executor.*
>
> *I appoint Ornette Coleman "L.A." Baron as my executor in all matters and require that no bond be required of him to serve as my representative and to dispose of my estate.*

L.A. signed it as Liam Raymond Nolan, dated it prior to Nolan's death, then crumpled and creased it until it looked worn. Next, he scanned it onto his desktop and deleted the history of the scan from his scanner.

He went through the usual security process on his computer, ending with changing his password and logged in to the Scribd document-sharing site. He uploaded the fake holographic will and labeled it *True Last Will and Testament of Liam Nolan.*

L.A. then wrote a blog with an interview by a supposedly well-known celebrity interviewer wherein Liam stated his value of and friendship with L.A. Baron. He further asserted that the will came from the office safe of Merit Bridges and that she had been hiding it all along to keep L.A. from controlling the estate.

Nolan was quoted as saying that he would never part with L.A. again, and wanted him to continue to run his affairs. The interview purportedly took place just prior to Nolan's death as part of his comeback plan. The catalyst for the re-post was the recently discovered holographic will and Merit's removal from the position as manager of the estate.

L.A. placed various tweets and Facebook postings linked to the fake blog and the holographic will.

"That should put the final nail in your coffin, Ms. Bridges. And maybe confuse the court as well," L.A. said to himself.

Val, dressed to the nines as usual, knocked on Merit's office door with several printed pages in hand.

"You're looking especially nice today." Merit said.

"Thanks. Went vintage shopping over the weekend. Found some real bargains," Val said.

"Good find," Merit said. "What do you have there?"

"I found this online. It's a will purportedly penned by Liam Nolan, but it's in cursive, not typed," Val said.

"It's probably more fake news, but let me take a look," Merit said.

Val gave her the pages and sat down. Merit read them while chewing on her lower lip.

"I can't believe Liam would have written this and not told me. He was very deliberate about putting his affairs in order," Merit said.

"It's not even printed or typed," Val said.

"A will doesn't have to be typed. It's holographic," Merit said.

"Got it," Val said. "We haven't studied holographic wills in class. What are the rules?"

"That's easy. There aren't many. The document must be completely handwritten by the testator and signed. It can be written on anything and doesn't have to be witnessed," Merit said.

"So just any piece of paper will do?" Val asked.

"It doesn't even have to be paper. There's an old case where a man wrote on his tractor, "All to Wife" and signed it. Another man who was in the hospital wrote on the wall next to his hospital bed "I leave everything to my wife" and signed the wall. Both were probated and passed the estates on to the wife. Clarity of intent is the key."

"That's all?" Val asked.

"Pretty much," Merit said. "The person must be legally competent to convey his wishes, but it helped that in both of those cases the wife inherited and no one challenged the writings."

"Was Liam in his right mind?" Val asked.

"I don't think anyone would question that Liam was sane. He was in NA, performing music around town, and working with us on the estate," Merit said.

"Right," Val said. "Why doesn't everyone just save the money and write a holographic will?"

"Case law is full of examples of complications with them. They are looked at with a questioning eye by the courts. Mostly, there are no tax benefits. Probate law is not only about bequeathing property, it's about saving do-re-mi from the IRS."

"How do we know if it's real," Val asked.

"I'm fairly certain it's not," Merit said. "Question is whether someone will present it to the probate court. If not, it's a hoax."

"What if they do?" Val asked.

"We call in handwriting experts. Show that Liam was in the process of a will here that was in contradiction to the holographic will. I'm betting it never surfaces. It's just a ploy to cast confusion and doubt."

"I hope you're right," Val said.

"What's interesting about it is that it puts L.A. in charge. Who would know about L.A. and his role in Liam's life? Who would put this out there?" Merit asked.

"I was pondering the same question," Val said.

"Where did you find this? Which site?" Merit asked.

"It was attached to an article saying you had been hiding the will in your safe," Val said.

Merit's armpits prickled severely.

"What?" Merit asked. "Is L.A. crazy enough to falsify documents? He's powerful and vulnerable to any scrutiny. He's a public figure. Please print all that out and email the site to me as well."

"Will do," Val said.

50

The next day, Gilbert Johnson entered the Law Office of Merit Bridges in his Sunday best. Merit came out to greet him with a warm handshake.

"Nice outfit," Merit said.

"I spent a few bucks," Gilbert said.

"Well, looks like you're going to have plenty of money for clothes soon. I got your title work back," Merit said.

She steered him into the conference room where Betty magically appeared with beverages and chocolate chip cookies.

I guess we're feeding the entire homeless population of Travis County, Merit thought.

Betty appeared to read her mind and smiled.

"I can sell the property now?" Gilbert said.

"Short answer, yes. Long answer, we need to clean up a few things around your Mom's deed and the title so that the new buyer can get proper title insurance," Merit said.

"Title insurance? How long will that take?" Gilbert asked. "The city keeps sending me these notices."

He presented an envelope to Merit with both hands. She opened it and read: NOTICE OF FORECLOSURE.

"I know some folks in the tax office," Merit said. "I've notified them that you are going to pay your taxes and they have agreed to delay collection until we get everything in order to sell. We should

227

be able to wrap this up in about three weeks or so. Then, you can close. The title company will pay your taxes and expenses out of your proceeds from the sale at closing."

"Three weeks?" Gilbert asked.

"We need to file the deed your mother gave to you so it is public record. It must process through the Travis County Clerk's office. That's where they keep all the property records. Then the title company can access the records and get your deed into the chain of title. That gets it into your name. Then you can sell it," Merit said.

"That's a lot of moving parts," Gilbert said.

"Not really. We do this all the time. I can have the title company file your Mother's deed for us so they are ahead of the paperwork when it finally comes back. You just need to let me know that it's okay to proceed," Merit said.

"Please, proceed," Gilbert said. "And, be sure the title company pays you too."

Merit smiled at him.

"Yes, sir!"

"By the by, I saw your friend at the St. John's Men's Shelter," Gilbert said. "Can't remember his name if I ever knew it."

"What friend?" Merit asked. "The only people I knew there were Liam and Davey. You know they're both gone."

"No, the new guy. He was listening to your education tapes," Gilbert said.

"What? What education tapes?" Merit said.

"That's what he told me they were," Gilbert said.

"Who? What are you talking about, Gilbert?" Merit asked.

"I went to the shelter for a meal and a shower. Remember, I don't have no electricity or water at my house. I was walking down the street over by the east door and I heard your voice in a big black SUV. A Cadillac I think," Gilbert said.

"My voice. Are you sure? You mean a recording?" Merit asked.

"Sure, I'm sure. I thought it was you so I poked my head in the window to say hello. You were on the radio talking about lawyer things," Gilbert said.

"Lawyer things? On the radio? What did I say?" Merit asked.

"Just law stuff about court and music money and stuff like that. There was a guy's voice too," Gilbert said. "You were explaining law to him."

"What did we say? Exactly. As much as you can remember," Merit asked.

"You said you wanted the man to research something," Gilbert said. "He was going to Llano or Lockhart, maybe Luling. Some place with an 'L'," Gilbert said.

"Did you ask the man why he was listening to my voice?" Merit asked.

"I did. He said he was studying educational tapes to learn about the law," Gilbert said.

"What did he look like?" Merit asked.

"He was a small skinny guy all in black. The SUV was black too with a funny license plate," Gilbert said.

"Do you remember the numbers or letters?" Merit asked.

"Something like music barn. It had a piano keyboard with notes floating out of it," Gilbert said. "It didn't have all the letters."

"Do you mean an acronym? A bunch of letters that stood for something else?" Merit asked.

"Yeah. It was like music without the U and Barn without the A," Gilbert said.

Merit wrote the letters on her legal pad: MSICBRN.

"That looks right," Gilbert said.

"Music baron," Merit said.

Merit hit the intercom button.

"Betty, could you come in right away, please?" Merit asked.

Betty entered and stood beside the desk with pad and pen at the ready.

"Please tell her what you told me," Merit said.

Gilbert repeated the gist of his experience.

Betty turned to Merit.

"When did you talk to Ag about going back to Llano?" Betty asked.

"That conversation was at six-thirty or so last Wednesday," Merit said.

"Gilbert, what time were you going into the shelter?" Betty asked.

"Dinnertime. I ate while I was there," Gilbert said. "Reverend Hightower and another guy came out to talk to the man in the SUV. The Reverend told me to go inside."

"Reverend Hightower? Liam's sponsor? Davey's guardian?" Betty said.

"Yep. He runs the shelter. The other guy always wears combat fatigues," Gilbert said.

"That's how he's doing it," Merit said. "He's listening to me in my office. How is that possible?"

Both Merit and Betty looked at the ceiling and the walls in the conference room. Gilbert looked up too.

"What are we looking for?" Gilbert asked.

"Let me get someone from Tech Security in here," Betty said.

"Now. Ag, too," Merit said.

"In one half less than no time," Betty said.

Merit and Gilbert looked at the walls and back at each other.

"Do you have bugs?" Gilbert asked.

♪

Ag went to see Chaplain after Merit's bout with the drowning of her BMW and Gilbert's revelation. After pleasantries and coffee, Ag got down to business.

"She barely made it out alive," Ag said.

"This new electronic terrorism using cars is just one more step up the ladder in cyberbullying. It's very hard to trace when a good hacker puts it into play. I don't know exactly how it works, but it's called rowhammering. Apparently it allows a hacker to hammer away at a certain row of transistors until a glitch occurs. Then they can sneak in through the glitch and get control of the protected level of the computer's operating system."

"I did some research, too. Apparently, the hackers can use a similar technique to go in through cloud computing services. All modern cars are somehow tied to the cloud by satellite radio, on-board security, that type of thing," Ag said.

"Scary stuff," Chaplain said.

"Deadly," Ag said.

"We'll reach out to BMW and see if we can get any leads back to the guilty party," Chaplain said.

"Thanks. I was hoping you would take that on," Ag said.

"Sounds like the same culprit who killed Davey Nolan," Chaplain said.

"We think so, too," Ag said.

"Know who it is?" Chaplain asked.

"All this time, we thought it might be about a big land deal going on out at Lake Travis near the Oasis. Now, we're pretty sure we've found the true culprit," Ag said.

"Let's hear it," Chaplain said.

"There's a guy in California who had a small stake in Liam Nolan's estate. Looks like that might be parlayed into something more valuable. Maybe in the millions," Ag said. "He's been appointed executor after Merit's removal."

"Give me his full name, I'll check him out and see what brand of snake oil he's selling," Chaplain said.

"He drives an Escalade with the license plate: MSICBRN and has an Austin office here in the Warehouse District," Ag said.

"Local. Even better," Chaplain said.

Merit, Betty, Ag, and Val sat in the big conference room in the Law Office of Merit Bridges. Betty served tea, coffee, and a fresh batch of homemade lemon squares with chocolate drizzle to the team. Merit opened the discussion.

"So, now we know it's been L.A. Baron ruining my reputation all along. Question is why." Merit said.

"I've advised Chaplain. My question is how do we put L.A. down like the lying dog he is?" Ag said.

"Easy, boy," Betty said.

"He almost killed her," Ag said.

Betty patted him on the shoulder.

"His time is coming," Betty said.

"Val has reports that *Fever Stomp* is rising in the charts in Asia," Merit said.

"When we got the ASCAP report forwarded from Liam's last address, I started to track his music in Japan," Val said. "At first it just looked like a small spike, but now it's slowly creeping up the charts."

"Box Office Japan has the song at number fifty-five. It's been used in a trailer promoting a film and has caught on in discos and all night dance clubs in Tokyo. I've also started following some new sources online and found that a company named TofuGrind has an online game coming and plans to follow up with a movie," Merit said. "They've used the song in their promos."

"Do we know that the song will be in the movie or the game?" Ag asked.

"No, but we can guess if they used it in the trailer, it might be," Merit said.

"As you know, L.A. Baron has the song under his management via his original contract with Liam," Val said.

"Putting two and two together," Betty said.

"Doesn't he have to report to the probate court?" Val asked.

"Yes and no. His rights under the contract don't expire with Liam's death, so he can continue to do business without permission as long as he properly compensates the estate. He takes his cut and passes on the rest," Merit said.

"But he hasn't been passing it along," Val said.

"Right. He's delayed the payments. All he needs to say is he was getting the quarterly income report together, blah blah. The court doesn't require immediate reporting, only reasonable reporting," Merit said. "He'll just say he hadn't gotten it done yet."

"We've used that trick," Val said.

"True," Betty said.

Merit winced.

"Under his contract, he only has management of about half a dozen songs left," Merit said. "The control of the others have expired, and the other six songs will too, unless they are in play."

"That's why he wants control of the probate," Ag said.

"That's his game. L.A.'s trying to snag Liam's music before the video game and movie come out," Merit said. "*Fever Stomp* could pull up Liam's entire portfolio into best seller status."

"He wants it badly enough to kill for it? There must be more than money behind it," Ag said.

"All this time, I assumed the estate was almost worthless. It's really a comeback story for Liam with a lot of money in play," Merit said.

"Also, he's next in line to control the probate for Davey now that Merit is discredited." Ag said.

"That's motive," Merit said.

"If he only has the one song, he will still make a lot of money on it," Val said.

"But he'll make more money if all of Liam's songs get popular again and L.A. has the entire portfolio," Merit said. "He gets a percentage of every dollar that goes through the estate, plus commission, plus expenses. More importantly, he gets the kudos, prestige and fame if he takes credit for the comeback. That's worth even more millions in the music biz."

"It wouldn't look so great for L.A. Baron if someone else took Liam's portfolio to the top when he couldn't or wouldn't do it," Ag said.

"Exactly. We need to get evidence. Something concrete that it's L.A. Baron," Merit said.

"Right. Something Chaplain can use," Ag said.

"If he's sunk to this level, he must have a history of bad acts. No one turns this evil overnight," Merit said.

"He's a real tool," Val said.

"If he swallowed a nail, he'd spit up a corkscrew," Betty said.

51

Merit sat in her condo looking out over downtown Austin and sipping a fall wine from DeLoach Winery. The phone rang with Ace's robot ringtone, so she picked it up.

"You're the only person who could have gotten me to answer the phone today," Merit said.

"Tough day?" Ace said.

"Just thinking," Merit said. "Is Ag's associate still watching over you?"

"Like a hawk. It makes me a celebrity. The girls like it," Ace laughed.

"Don't give him the slip. It's probably unnecessary, but just in case," Merit said.

"I'm not scared. I know what's going on, Mom," Ace said.

"Well, try to keep your focus on school," Merit said. "Remember what Johnny Depp says, just do what you have to do for you."

"Right, and keep moving forward. Being dyslexic doesn't keep you from knowing that," Ace said.

"Just be careful," Merit said.

"I called to tell you something. Just listen, Mom. I saw some pictures online and it gave me an idea," Ace said.

"What type of pictures? You're not looking at porn are you?" Merit laughed.

"No, Mom. It's online where my group posts our Pokémon pictures that we take while playing the game," Ace said.

"Sounds fun. How does it work?" Merit asked.

"It's easy, Mom. You just use the Pokémon Go app on your phone," Ace said.

"I don't have a Pokémon Go app," Merit said.

"Pretend you do. You're at UT walking around the Littlefield Fountain. You're catching wild Pokémon characters like Eevee or Charizard," Ace said.

"There are wild ones? I thought they were on cards," Merit said.

"They are, but they're also on the app. Just listen, Mom. Let's say you find Eevee, my favorite. You snap a pic and Eevee shows up on the screen sitting on the edge or standing around where the fountain is the background."

"I think I get it. Coolio," Merit said.

"It's just part of the game of catching Pokémon around town," Ace said.

"That sounds entertaining, but what is the idea?" Merit asked.

"There are pictures taken all over Austin every day. There were photos taken on the night Liam was killed. I checked the date. And, there are some around Lady Bird Lake and the First Street Bridge," Ace said.

Merit stood up. Her armpits prickled as she grasped the significance of what Ace was saying.

"Really? There aren't pictures of Liam being killed are there?"

"No, not that, but there are pictures of tons of people walking around and even some in the middle of the night," Ace said.

"Can you tell anything by the photos about who might have been down there?" Merit asked.

"No, I don't recognize anybody. But, you might be able to take them to the police and see if they can enhance them. It would at least show who was out at that hour," Ace said.

"How many photos are we talking about?" Merit asked.

"Hundreds. I can't get into other people's photos, just my group, but the police could. I'm sure there are more floating around. Could be thousands of groups with similar pictures."

"You are a genius! What a great idea," Merit said.

"Dyslexics think outside the box," Ace said. "Just ask Einstein, Steve Jobs or Tom Cruise."

"Absolutely, but only Cruise is alive to ask. And you, of course," Merit laughed. "Can you send me some links or copies of some of the information you're talking about?" Merit asked.

"Just sent you the group login. You might have to make a fake Avatar or something to join the Pokémon group. I'd hate to see my old Mom on my gaming site," Ace laughed.

"Watch it," Merit said.

♪

Merit and Ag sat outside near the bandstand at Threadgill's drinking long neck beers and listening to Black Joe Lewis and the Honeybears croon a familiar tune. Derek O'Brien sat in on drums. In the corner, Lucinda Williams prepared to take the stage next. Through the glass, a mural of Janis Joplin and Kenneth Threadgill watched over the music lovers and home cooking diners.

Merit leaned in and spoke into Ag's ear.

"I wanted to meet in a noisy place where we can't be heard because I want to talk to you about something," Merit said.

Ag snapped to attention.

"There's not much you keep from Betty and Val. What's up?" Ag said.

"I hired a blackhat hacker to try to find a link to who's been trying to take me down," Merit said. "I know it's L.A., we just can't prove it. I wanted you to have…"

"Plausible deniability. I did the same thing. The trail is not traceable. We've tried everything. They must be using evasive techniques every time they login," Ag said.

"Well, you sneaky bastard," Merit laughed. "I figured out the same thing. We could go for a bit and then the trail would dry up,"

Ag winked at her.

"Who do you think you are? Perry Mason?" Ag asked.

"More like Ally McBeal," Merit laughed.

"Ok, so now we've come clean about our criminal acts. What's next?" Ag asked.

"I got a call from Ace with a crazy idea that might just work. It won't help us catch the hacker, but it might lead us to Liam's killer and they're probably one and the same," Merit said.

"L.A. Baron? A murderer?" Ag asked.

"That's my guess, unless Davey was the devil in disguise, or Louellen lost her marbles and threw a hissy fit," Merit said.

"Jeez. He's so visible to the public," Ag said and took a long pull on his frosty longneck.

"So is every child molester and wife beater we've ever met," Merit said.

"True," Ag said.

"I had my hacker try something else based on the idea Ace had," Merit said.

"What did he come up with?" Ag asked.

"Ace suggested we check out this new kid's game called Pokémon Go. The players run around snagging awards and pictures of their favorite characters to build up points in the game. They play in groups that they're assigned to by the game coordinators," Merit said.

"How does it help us?" Ag asked.

"We hacked into all the Pokémon Go groups around the U.S. and pulled all the pictures of people who were visiting Austin on the night of Liam's murder," Merit said.

"Pokémon? The game?"

"Exactly. That's what I said when Ace introduced the idea. Apparently, part of the game is to snap pics in these touristy areas and pretend that a Pokémon is alive on site and visiting with you," Merit said.

"And you got all the pictures without a warrant?" Ag asked.

"I'm not trying to convict anyone. The police can go back and get them legally if they want. I just need to see who did it," Merit said. "Most of it is open to the public anyway."

"Mmm hmm."

♪

Ag and Chaplain sat in Ag's office with Ag's laptop set up between them. They were moving through thousands of Pokémon pictures and video in fast motion.

"See, it's just like the old flip or flick books. I used it old school on that case I had about the doctor that was killed. There's software that does it now," Ag said.

"What am I looking at?" Chaplain asked.

"It's a game the kids play with an app on their phone called Pokémon Go," Ag said.

"Where was this taken and why am I looking at it?" Chaplain said.

"It's the area around Lady Bird Lake on the night of Liam's murder." Ag said.

"Where did you get these?" Chaplain asked.

"Off the internet," Ag said.

"Mmm hmm," Chaplain said.

"Just watch," Ag said.

Ag clicked around the screen and zeroed in on a set of photos of Lakeshore Boulevard and clips from the videos of Davey walking over the pedestrian bridge and down the hike and bike path at night.

"This is about an hour before time of death," Ag said. "See the time stamp on this footage?"

Davey walked past the First Street Bridge, down the path past the high traffic area, and disappeared out of the video. Next, Ag cued up three still shots. The two teenagers with the drones were in and out of the photos.

"So, we already knew Davey was down there," Chaplain said.

"Yes, but we didn't know that he had already left the area when Liam was killed," Ag said.

"He could have come back," Chaplain said.

"True. But, watch this," Ag said.

Davey did not re-appear, and the two teenagers were no longer in the pictures either. A forty-eight-minute gap showed on the timer before the next picture appears. The flip stopped and only two photos were present onscreen.

"No one took video or a picture for a while. It was the middle of the night," Ag said. "But then, here are just two showing something around the time of Liam's murder."

"What is that?" Chaplain said.

"Looks like someone approaching the bridge. Liam must have already been under it based on the time of death and the time stamp on the picture," Ag said.

"That is a small man. Could be Davey. Maybe a woman. I can't tell with the dark and grainy photo," Chaplain said.

"Neither can I, but this person has on different clothes than Davey. He could have changed, but Davey was sleeping in the woods. Not likely he changed clothes," Ag said.

"Agreed. This cap has an insignia I can't read. Hard to make out a face," Chaplain said. "Did you try to enhance it?"

"Yes. This is the best we could get, but when I zoom in, you can see just the last letters on the cap and a mark or tattoo on the person's right arm. Looks like a man to me," Ag said.

"Agreed. I think it's a man," Chaplain said.

"Any ideas how to get more information out of this?" Ag said.

"I might have a connection or two with a little better equipment than your hacker," Chaplain said.

"Hacker? Who said anything about a hacker?" Ag said.

Chaplain rolled his eyes.

52

Merit, Betty, and Ag stood outside the law office in the hallway by the glass doors. Merit and Ag were holding small silver boxes with a wire coming out of the side and attached to a thin pencil type wand.

"You know we had this done a while back," Betty said.

"Someone or something must have gotten in here or they missed it when they checked before," Ag said. "I bought this equipment at the recommendation of Tech Security so we can sweep every day."

"No one has been in her office alone since the sweep except for Val and me," Betty said to Ag. "You checked all the video tapes and I double checked them just to be sure."

"Someone is listening to us," Merit said. "I was sitting at my desk when I talked to Ag about going back to Llano. There's no bug on my phone. We've checked and re-checked. My computer is clear. It has to be in there somewhere."

"When we go in there, we don't talk about what we're doing. Got it?" Ag said.

"Yep," Betty said.

The three entered the glass doors and went down the hall to Merit's office. Merit and Ag moved around the room in tandem with the two high tech boxes in their hands. Each held the wand and both passed them over and around furniture, walls, paintings, and rugs. Betty stood at the door watching the two. They looked like humming birds buzzing around a plant, stopping to sample a bit here, a little more there.

Merit wanded over to Betty.

"Are you a spy?" Merit mouthed and swept the wand over Betty with a grin on her face.

"You got me," Betty said laughing.

Merit swept past Betty and the door to the other wall and the small silver box began to click. She swept back and the click became louder.

Betty's jaw dropped. "What the hell?" she asked.

"Check your clothes," Merit mouthed and pointed to Betty's pockets.

Betty patted the pockets, the hem of her skirt and the cuffs on her blouse. Ag came over and started wanding her as well. The sound became stronger when he moved over to the edge of the open door. Merit pulled Betty in by the hand and closed the door. Merit wanded the door and settled with the loudest clicks on the boxing gloves.

Merit and Betty looked at each other.

"The gift," Merit mouthed the words.

"Shhh," Ag said and put his finger to his lips.

"I guess we better get back to work," Merit said in her normal voice.

"I bet the mail has been delivered by now," Betty said.

"Yeah, I've got a lot to do," Ag said.

They all three went out into the hallway and closed the door quietly behind them.

53

Merit pulled the Texas Probate Code and flipped to Section 59. She read quietly as she walked down the hall to Val's office.

"Hi, Merit. What's up?" Val said with his hand poised over an iPad.

"Put that away if it hasn't been checked by Tech Security," Merit said.

Val put down the iPad and picked up a legal pad and designer pen.

"Ready," Val said.

"We're going to need to file another probate. This one is for Davey Ray Nolan a/k/a Davey Ray Bell," Merit said. "Attach a copy of the short will that Davey signed and Betty put in the safe. Return the original to her after you copy it so she can lock it up again."

"Can do," Val said. "What about Davey and Liam both being dead at the same time?"

"We know that Davey died more than one hundred and twenty hours after Liam."

"What does one hundred and twenty hours have to do with it?" Val asked.

"It's called a survivorship period and is partially a tax thing. To inherit under Texas' intestate succession statutes, a person must outlive the other dead person by one hundred and twenty hours," Merit said.

"What difference does that make?" Val said.

"Say Liam and Davey had been in a car wreck together and Davey died a few hours after Liam. It's treated as one event. It prevents going through probate for a double death and saves the family paying the inheritance tax twice," Merit said.

"Interesting," Val said and wrote some notes on his legal pad.

"That's not our problem. We need to show Davey would never have used L.A. Baron as his executor. Just start a form and I'll tweak it. Don't send it to me in email. With all that's going on around here, let's do this very carefully. Use only your desktop and work with the document on the office portal. Tech Security has cleared that," Merit said. "I'll log into the portal and work there as well."

♪

Merit and Val sat at the attorney's table on one side of the Probate Court of Travis County, Judge Madeline Herman presiding, and L.A. sat across the aisle with his attorney Blake Tipton.

"We have several topics on the agenda today," Judge Herman said. "Let's start with you, Mr. Tipton."

Tipton stood with a document in his hand. He looked over at the court reporter to make sure the stenographer was typing and his words would be on the record.

"Your Honor," Tipton said. "This document is a holographic will in the handwriting of Liam Nolan according to our experts. It was sent by U.S. mail to my client, Mr. Baron. We'd like to enter it into the probate records as the Last Will and Testament of Liam Nolan.

Merit was on her feet. "Objection. Judge, there is no way Liam Nolan executed a holographic will in the midst of his work with my office. We have no way of knowing if this document is real or not."

"It will be a battle of the experts to authenticate it," Tipton said.

L.A. smirked.

"Experts can be bought, Your Honor. Besides, the will is moot," Merit said.

Tipton was on his feet. "A will cannot be moot unless it is authenticated or disproved as to authorship."

"Just a minute Mr. Tipton. Continue, Ms. Bridges," Judge Herman said.

Merit took a page from a file and lifted it for all to see.

"Your Honor," Merit said. "A copy of this will of Davey Ray Nolan a/k/a Davey Ray Bell was filed with the original probate just moments before this hearing. I surrender this original to the court for safekeeping. It surpasses Liam Nolan's will as Davey Ray Nolan is his only heir."

"Objection. We have no way of knowing if this document is real or not," Tipton said.

"What is the history of this document, Ms. Bridges?" Judge Herman asked.

"It was prepared in my office prior to Davey Ray Nolan's death," Merit said.

Merit picked up a file from the table and pulled out another document.

"I present a sworn affidavit by my office manager, indicating that Davey Ray Nolan signed the will in her presence as notary on the date indicated. She also affirms that the will has been in my office safe since that day," Merit said.

Merit picked up a third file and removed a thick report.

"This document is an analysis of Davey Ray Nolan's handwriting. It is signed by Cho Liu of Liu Handwriting Experts and authenticates the signature as being Davey Ray Nolan's."

Merit handed Tipton a file containing copies of the documents.

"Objection. Your Honor, there's a lot of inference here. We have not had an opportunity to examine these documents and have our experts authenticate them." Tipton said.

"Mr. Tipton, we'll take them at face value for now. You can have your experts look at them and if you find any irregularities, file a new motion and set a hearing," Judge Herman said.

The judge flipped through the documents and the case law Merit provided.

"I'm going to accept the will for probate. If you want to file a civil suit to challenge its authenticity, you're welcome to do so. For now, we'll proceed with probate," Judge Herman said.

"Thank you, Your Honor," Merit said.

L.A. tensed his jaw.

Tipton stood up.

"Your Honor, Ms. Bridges has been removed from the administration of this estate due to her lack of veracity and questionable ethics practices," Tipton said. "Further, Ms. Bridges is being investigated for embezzlement of funds from Texas KnockOut Illiteracy. The organization has accepted her resignation, which I believe was forced upon her."

"If I may, Your Honor?" Merit asked.

The judge looked knowingly at her and nodded.

"This is a new probate. Although it contains the same property as the estate of Liam Nolan, the property has passed through that probate and is now in the estate of Davey Ray Nolan. He did not die intestate as did his father. He had the right to appoint an executor of his choosing in his will to administer the estate. None of the allegations Mr. Tipton raises have been proved against me. Davey Ray Nolan chose me and the court does not have the discretion to question his testamentary plan under these circumstances," Merit said.

"That's correct, Ms. Bridges," Judge Herman said. "If Davey Ray Nolan trusted you to handle his affairs, that's enough for this court for now. I'll be keeping abreast of things."

L.A. avoided eye contact with Tipton.

"Davey Ray Nolan cannot benefit from a death he caused. He is still under suspicion for killing his father," Mr. Tipton said.

Merit pulled another document from the folder.

"May I approach, Your Honor?" Merit asked.

The judge curled her fingers signaling permission. Merit handed the document to the judge and a copy to Mr. Tipton.

"This document is signed by Detective Chaplain of the APD. It indicates that Davey Ray Nolan has been cleared post mortem of any wrongdoing in the case of his father's death. It elaborates on evidence showing his whereabouts at the time of the murder. His alibi has been deemed solid," Merit said.

L.A. jerked his head up and gripped the table. The judge looked at the report from Chaplain.

"This appears to be in order. The estate passes to Davey Ray Nolan and Ms. Bridges is hereby appointed executor of his estate. Ms. Bridges, file all this paperwork and set up new accounts. I still want regular reporting on all expenditures and activities," the judge said.

"Yes, Your Honor," Merit breathed a sigh of relief.

L.A. stood up. Tipton put a hand on L.A.'s shoulder and pushed him back down into his seat.

"Court adjourned," the judge said and slammed down the gavel.

♪

After the probate hearing, L.A. returned to his office and began to throw files and all the burner phones into a moving box. His hands were shaking as he fed several sheets of paper through a shredder. He deleted several documents from his computer and emptied the trash. He stopped and clinched his fists but when he opened his hands, they were still shaking. He went over to the bar, poured a shot of gin, and downed it in one gulp.

He looked over at the closet door and back at the box of evidence of his wrong doing and loss. He knew there really was no choice.

He walked across the room, unlocked and opened the sanctuary door, went in, and sat on the stool. He began his ritualistic chanting.

"I'm so sorry. I'm so sorry. Dahl forgive me. My brother, please forgive me. Please forgive me."

He began to grind his teeth until he heard a popping in his jaw. The wail he expressed was higher than the decibels at any of his rock concerts.

"Aaaahhhhh!"

54

Merit and Ag entered the St. John's Men's Shelter and looked around for Reverend Hightower. He was using a large ladle to pour soup into ceramic bowls and passing them down the line to shelter volunteers and staff who in turn took them to the picnic style tables. Dozens of men were waiting patiently to hear grace and have dinner.

Reverend Hightower looked up and saw Merit and Ag.

"Let us bow our heads in prayer," Reverend Hightower boomed above the noise.

The room became quiet. Merit and Ag stopped where they were and bowed their heads along with everyone else. Merit kept one eye on Reverend Hightower as he delivered the prayer before the meal.

"Lord, bless this food for the nourishment of our bodies. We ask Thee to keep us on the diligent path of awareness in all we say and do. Protect us in our wrong doing and deliver us from our enemies. In Jesus' name, Amen."

As soon as the prayer was complete, Reverend Hightower slipped behind the serving line and moved toward his office door.

Merit and Ag never lost sight of him and followed not far behind. They came to the closed door with a sign that said *OFFICE* on it. Merit tried it, but it was locked. She nodded at Ag and he reared back and kicked the door in.

The office was empty. The exit door to the parking lot was ajar and Reverend Hightower was nowhere to be seen. Merit looked out the door to dust settling in the parking lot.

Merit and Ag went back out into the dining area and looked around. There were several men in army fatigues, but only one with a hundred-dollar haircut.

Merit took her phone from her pocket, looked down at it, then up at Ag. He nodded. Ag picked up a plate from the serving table and dropped it. All eyes in the room went to Ag. Merit snapped a picture of the man in fatigues and expensive haircut without his knowledge.

♪

Merit sat at her glass dining table sipping a red blend and looking through a sheaf of papers with the letterhead of Tech Security at the top. The report covered all the checks Tech Security had done on Merit's office room by room. Except for the boxing gloves, there was nothing else active in any of the offices, on her phones, or on any of the office computers. Upon advice of Tech Security, she had forbidden the use of laptops at home until the leaks were plugged. She felt fairly confident that she was no longer being monitored.

Merit opened an additional report in a plain manila envelope and read dates and figures hacked from the bank statements of the St. John's Men's Shelter and the private account of Reverend Morton Hightower.

"This hacker is worth every penny," she said and whistled.

Merit scanned the chronology finding an influx of cash over the past six months. She also checked the day of her visit to the shelter with Ag. On that date, Reverend Hightower had withdrawn all the cash from his private account totaling over one hundred thousand dollars. The withdrawal information showed he had taken the funds in hundreds and twenties.

"Not bad for a wing and a prayer," Merit said.

She hit the favorites button on her phone and autodialed Ag's mobile number.

"Hey you," Ag said.

"Hi there. I'll speak in code because we're on a mobile. Remember that report I asked our Tech Security buddies to prepare?" Merit asked.

"Say no more. I'm with you," Ag said.

"I think we ran our shelter buddy out of town," Merit said.

"Yep. I was afraid of that," Ag said.

♪

Merit and Ag arrived at APD and waited for Chaplain. He came out of his office to greet them and took them into a room set up for viewing interviews in the adjoining room.

"We snagged Ash Joyner on his way out of town after your little drama at the men's shelter. He's lawyered up," Chaplain said.

"We would have given you a head's up if we'd known Hightower was going to rabbit," Ag said.

"We caught them both, so no harm, no foul. We need more to charge Hightower than money in his bank account," Chaplain said. "People donate to that shelter all the time, although the personal deposits are suspect."

"You think?" Ag said.

"He's right," Merit said. "It's not enough."

"Let's take a shot at Ash Joyner. See if he can give us some leverage over Hightower. Please remain here and silent. You're watching this as a courtesy," Chaplain said and left the room.

"A courtesy because we solved the case," Ag said. "We brought him the photo of Ash Joyner."

Merit smiled. "Let's finish it," she said.

They sat in metal chairs facing the standard police department two-way mirrored wall and watched Chaplain in the next room. He sat across from the man with the expensive haircut now known to them as Ash Joyner and another man who was identified as Joyner's attorney. Merit recognized the lawyer from the criminal bar as Joe Baggett.

"Ash Joyner doesn't look like a murderer," Merit said.

"Wasn't it you who said they rarely do?" Ag asked.

Merit made a face at Ag and turned up the volume on the speaker beside the glass.

"For the record, you are here of your own volition. You have your attorney present and you've been advised of your rights," Chaplain said to Ash.

"Yes," Ash said.

"Hold it, Baggett said. "My client will agree to give you full information in exchange for a suspended sentence on all counts."

"Suspended for murder? You've got to be kidding," Chaplain said.

"I didn't murder anybody," Ash said.

Baggett put a hand on Ash's arm.

Chaplain went out the door and came back with Assistant D.A. Sandra Blanton.

"Mr. Joyner wants a deal," Chaplain said.

"If one word is a lie, the deal is going away for good. If you did not kill Liam Nolan or Davey Ray Nolan, and you give us who did, we'll recommend suspended.

In the adjoining room, Ag said, "Let's see if this asshole can tell the truth."

"He looks scared enough," Merit said. "What does he have to lose?"

"Who killed them?" Chaplain said.

"I don't know about Liam," Ash said. "I assume it was L.A. or Louellen Bell. I do know that Davey Ray Nolan was killed via a method used by an L.A. techie named HackerDude. I don't know his real name. I also heard a conversation between L.A. and Reverend Hightower arranging for Davey to borrow the car. I helped set him up to ask for it when he needed to see his attorney."

"Did you know they were going to kill him?" Chaplain said.

"I guessed. What else would they be doing?" Ash said.

"That's conspiracy to commit murder," Blanton said.

"Do we have a deal?" Baggett asked.

"What about me?" Merit said to the glass. "They tried to get me too."

"Did you know they were going after the attorney, Merit Bridges?" Chaplain asked.

"He heard you," Ag said.

Merit laughed.

"I didn't know until after when I put two and two together," Ash said. "HackerDude set up listening devices in Bridges office and on her phone. They lost the phone bug after a while, but they are still listening to the office."

"That's what you think," Merit said.

Chaplain joined Merit and Ag and left Blanton to work out the plea details.

"Wonder how we can find this HackerDude," Ag said.

"We'll put out the word, but these guys are hard to find and we don't even have a real name," Chaplain said.

"If we can find him, maybe he'll turn on L.A. too," Ag said.

"Revenge of the nerd," Merit said.

55

Merit arrived at the offices of the State Bar of Texas without an attorney. She had decided to go against common wisdom and represent herself. Merit knew it was a gamble with her law license at stake, but she trusted her gut. She had on her navy Neiman Marcus suit and white pumps. She carried her lucky briefcase, which was a gift from Woody when she had opened her own firm.

She approached the reception desk.

"Merit Bridges here for the two o'clock hearing," she said.

After a short wait in some very uncomfortable straight-back chairs, Merit was called into a conference room before a bank of three of her peers.

The chairman of the committee said, "Please sit."

Merit smoothed her skirt with both hands and sat in the chair before the tribunal.

"As you know, this complaint was filed by Louellen Bell. She has not yet arrived. We are prepared to hear your statement," the chairman said.

Merit cleared her throat and steadied herself.

"As you are aware from my written response, I have been the victim of an attack on my character by L.A. Baron, my opponent in a heavily contested probate battle. I believe that Ms. Bell's actions here may have been instigated by Mr. Baron. Regardless, I owe no obligation to Ms. Bell, as I do not believe her to be an heir to the estate. She's offered no proof of a common law marriage to Liam

Nolan. My investigator is in the process of creating a time line showing that she could not have been married to him at the time she asserts," Merit said.

"Anything further?" the chairman asked.

"Yes. Even if Ms. Bell were proven to be an heir, I have acted with the utmost care and in an ethical manner toward all interested parties. If she meets the probate court criterion to inherit half of the estate of Liam Nolan, leaving Davey Ray Nolan's estate the other half, I will administer the estate in keeping with that ruling," Merit said.

Merit thought of the illegal hacking she had authorized but didn't mention that.

"So noted. Since the complainant, Louellen Bell, has failed to appear to give testimony today, we will withhold our ruling. We will continue to try to reach her to ascertain her current interest in pursuing the complaint and then advise you of the outcome of the investigation," the chairman said.

Louellen entered the Law Office of Merit Bridges wearing a new dress and spiked heels. She walked up to Mai, the receptionist. Louellen's boyfriend and bodyguard sat in the chair closest to the door and remained silent.

"I'm Louellen Bell. Here to see Merit Bridges."

Merit and Betty watched through the glass wall from the conference room.

"She must be expecting something. Looks like she's wearing a new dress," Merit said.

"Lipstick on a pig," Betty said.

"The worst mother I've seen in a long while," Merit said.

"Abandoning that boy to the street. Shameful," Betty said.

"Poor Davey. Amazing that he did as well as he did with no father and that for a mother," Merit said.

"You're taking a real chance that you'll have to pay her out of pocket if the probate court doesn't approve the expenditure. Are you sure you don't want to wait?" Betty asked.

"No," Merit said. "I'm betting on me."

"I am too, Darlin'," Betty smiled.

Mai showed Louellen into the conference room and Merit indicated a chair on the long side of the table.

"How about some coffee?" Merit said.

"How would you like it?" Betty asked.

"Black please, two sugars," Louellen said

"You need it," Betty mumbled as she left the room.

Seemingly oblivious to the slight, Louellen looked at Merit.

Merit took a seat at the head of the table and opened a file. She set a thick document before Louellen.

"This document settles all matters between you, Davey's estate, Liam's estate, Liam's music, and this law firm. It prevents you from writing, speaking or singing about them, me or your interactions with them or me in any way," Merit said.

"What do I get?" Louellen asked.

"What you get is the sum of money set forth on page one. It settles your involvement with the estate in the entirety. If you want to take time to have an attorney review the document, I'll be happy to give you a few days," Merit said.

"Nah, I can read," Louellen said.

"Then initial on page four that you were offered an opportunity to confer with counsel and declined," Merit said.

"Got it," Louellen said.

"On page four, there's a clause that says that this payment in no way influences your statements or actions with regard to the State Bar of Texas," Merit said. "Initial there."

"So they won't think you're buying me off?" Louellen initialed in the blank provided.

Merit didn't flinch.

"On page five you'll see that you are required to cooperate fully and honestly with Detective Chaplain and APD. Whatever they need. You acknowledge that this payment is in no way connected to your statements to the police or any testimony you may later give," Merit said.

"I gave them my forwarding address already," Louellen said.

Merit pressed the intercom for Betty to come in.

While they waited for Betty, Merit pulled an envelope from her desk but kept it near her on the table. The cellophane window showed that it was made out to Louellen Bell. Louellen looked at the envelope and almost salivated.

Betty entered with a notary book and a stamp.

"Please acknowledge this signature, Betty," Merit said.

Betty turned to Louellen.

"Sign on the last page and again here in my notary book, then raise your right hand," Betty said.

Louellen signed twice and raised her hand.

"Do you affirm that you are Louellen Bell," Betty said.

"I do," Louellen said.

"Do you assert that the statements in this document are true to the best of your knowledge and belief, and that you have executed this document knowingly and willingly for the purposes and consideration therein expressed?" Betty asked.

"I do," Louellen said and dropped her hand.

Betty signed her name below Louellen's, stamped the notary seal beside her signature, gathered up her notary kit, and left the room.

Merit pushed the envelope with the check over to Louellen, but did not take her hand from it.

"You have agreed never to contact me again. If you do, the contract requires you to repay all the money. I can sue you in court for anything you have or will ever have again. Do you understand?" Merit asked.

"I can read," Louellen said.

Merit waited.

"Yeah, I understand," said Louellen.

Merit pushed the check over to Louellen. She snatched it up, put it in her purse and headed for the door.

"Thanks a lot," Louellen said.

Merit squeezed her fist and did not respond.

After Louellen left, Betty entered with a cup of tea for Merit.

"To soothe the taste of bile," Betty said.

"What happened to the coffee for Louellen?" Merit said.

"It's still brewing, I guess," Betty shrugged.

"She won't be back," Merit said.

"Wonder how long it will take her to go through the cash. Too much money if you ask me," Betty asked

"Enough to cut off the malignancy and get rid of her for good. Last thing we need is ten years of litigation with that bitch," Merit said.

"She's just like a pimple. I'd like to pop her." Betty said.

"She's officially popped," Merit said.

Two APD officers stood outside the glass office doors in the building hallway and took Louellen into custody as she left.

"You're under arrest for conspiracy in the murder of Davey Ray Nolan," one officer said.

Louellen's boyfriend and bodyguard had disappeared.

Louellen looked back over her shoulder at Merit and mouthed the word, "Bitch."

Betty laughed.

"We've taken care of the estate. The police can handle the rest," Merit said.

56

Merit arrived in the lobby of her high rise and checked the TV screen above the reception desk for her unit number. It showed dry cleaning and two packages were waiting for her. She asked the doorman for her items and ripped open the FedEx package while she waited for him to obtain the dry cleaning from the laundry service room.

A copy of a microfiche news story from the St. Louis Post was in the envelope along with a brief note from a landman she'd hired in St. Louis to do some checking on L.A. Baron. She'd googled L.A.'s name, but had not found what she was looking for. There was the usual local boy makes good, but nothing about his childhood or early life. To go deeper she'd had to bring in some local help, and it had paid off. The note indicated that the one news story was all the investigator had found in St. Louis. However, the Post story led the investigator to two other news stories in Jackson, Wyoming.

Merit sat down on the sofa in the lobby and read the articles. They told the story of Ornette Coleman Baron and his twin brother, Dahl Burnett Baron, who was two minutes older than L.A.

Apparently, they had been hiking alone while on a family vacation in Wyoming when they were seventeen years old. Dahl was reported to have fallen to his death from a ledge at the side of the trail. Foul play was suspected but could not be proven due to the numerous contusions from falling against sharp rocks.

Dahl was reported to have been a natural musician with perfect pitch who could pick up any instrument and play it with little effort. He had just formed a garage band with several of his buddies and was thought to be the next rock star. He had been accepted as a guest on Amateur Music Hour, a predecessor to American Idol.

Ornette Coleman Baron could shed no light on the accident and had fallen into a deep depression. He had been hospitalized for over a year before he was able to return to school.

The third article was a twenty-year anniversary story on Dahl Baron's death. It reported that the case had never been completely solved to the satisfaction of local authorities.

The investigator indicated in his letter that the hospital where Ornette Coleman Baron was housed used many controversial techniques for rehabilitation, including light deprivation therapy. None of the techniques led to a confession or any information that would solve the mystery of the death of Dahl Baron.

It was revealed that Ornette Coleman Baron's aspirations toward becoming the music talent that his brother had been were never realized due to his lack of aptitude. He was reported to have gone into the business side of the music industry.

A photo from a high school yearbook showed the two boys. As they stood together, Dahl was a full foot taller than L.A. Further examination of the photo showed matching tattoos of music notes on their right arms.

I've seen that before, Merit thought. *On the arm of the suspect from the Pokémon photos.*

"You've used a rock to solve your problems before," Merit said.

L.A. sat in his Austin office for hours without moving from his chair. He could feel the dogs closing in on him. All his bad acts nipped at his heels and the loud barking filled his mind with such noise he couldn't think. He knew the police were going to put things together now that the shelter had been raided and Ash Joyner arrested.

He needed a plan to escape the dogs but his logical mind would not click into problem solving mode. His grip on reality lessened even further when the telephone rang and he jumped from his chair. He looked at the phone as if it were alive, turned, and ran to the closet. He fumbled with the code several times before he was able to open the lock. When he did, he ran inside and slammed the door behind him and rammed the lock. He did not sit on the stool, but rushed to the corner and slid down the wall to the floor.

He begged Dahl for forgiveness, then Liam, then God.

"I'm sorry Dahl. I'm so sorry. Please forgive me Liam. Dear God, please don't send me to the Land of Nod," L.A. said again and again.

♪

Merit arrived at the Austin State Hospital with Ag. They checked in with the receptionist and waited for L.A.'s doctor to come out. A graying man in a white coat came out to greet them. His name tag said Dr. Walker.

"You're not going to be able to see him," Dr. Walker said.

"I figured as much," Merit said.

"Why was Merit asked to come here?" Ag asked.

"There were some lucid moments at first, but those have disappeared. Mr. Baron has gone into a dark place in his mind and will probably never come out. Regardless, he'll be here at ASH for a long time."

"Thank you, Dr. Walker," Merit said.

Both Merit and Ag shook his hand and he went back through the door from which he'd arrived.

"Well, that's that," Ag said. "Chaplain said when they arrested L.A., he kept mumbling about the Land of Nod."

"Really? Like Cain in the Bible. God sent him to wander in the Land of Nod for killing his brother Abel."

"I guess you'll never get a chance to confront him for what he's done to you and your reputation," Ag said.

"I can still sue his estate for defamation of character. Maybe get some extra money for the charities Davey set up with Liam's money," Merit said.

"Revenge?" Ag asked.

"Seems empty, doesn't it?" Merit said. "He'd never know anyway, he's so out of it."

"True," Ag said.

"One small consolation, the record sales have gone through the roof with all this bad publicity," Merit said. "Makes my job wrapping up the contract with TofuGrind a lot sweeter."

"Crazy. In the end, you got just what L.A. was trying to prevent," Ag said.

"Coolio," Merit said.

57

Betty brought a stack of mail into Merit's office and put it on her desk.

"You might want to look at that top letter right away," Betty said.

"What?" Merit asked.

Merit read silently.

"Well, nice to have some good news for a change," Merit said.

"It's a great day in Austin," Betty said.

"Since Louellen Bell failed to appear to give testimony and could not be reached, I'm cleared with the State Bar and the file is officially closed."

"I think this calls for some Blue Bell Vanilla Bean." Betty said.

"I'm thinking Malbec," Merit said.

Merit and Betty worked several long days setting up the Liam and Davey Nolan Arts Foundation. The charities that had been listed in both wills were used as a list for recipients.

After the news broke of L.A.'s orchestrated attack on Merit's good name, Global Financial and most of Merit's top clients slowly returned to her client base.

Merit was invited back on the board of Knock Out Illiteracy but declined to accept. She wanted some time to sort through her life and get her priorities in order before she took on another task that large.

A few clients would not swallow their pride and apologize, but Merit didn't miss them much.

"Looks like we lost Mrs. Ranker," Betty said.

"She'll have her diamonds to keep her warm," Merit laughed.

Gilbert sold his property and Merit helped him set up bank accounts to protect his proceeds.

On a beautiful Texas day, Merit, her staff, and a handful of Austin dignitaries and music friends stood on the banks of Lady Bird Lake where Liam had been slain by L.A. It seemed eons since the night of the festival. Merit had been changed. They had all been changed by the events surrounding the now world famous guitarist and his abandoned son.

Red Thallon stood a respectable distance away but had her cameraman zoom in on the proceedings.

The attendees formed a half moon circle around a tall statue which was covered by a sheet. Merit stood beside it.

"Liam Raymond Nolan was not a perfect man, but he was a good man," Merit said. "His son Davey Ray Nolan had a good heart too. His last wishes were for the establishment of a foundation to support music in Austin. Although he did not specify this statue, he did specify that his father be honored in some way. This is that way."

Merit pulled the end of the sheet until it released and fell from the statue of Liam Ray Nolan with his guitar around his neck. The figure was all iron except for a purple guitar pick in its fingers. The base was inset with a plaque that read: *In Honor of Liam Raymond Nolan from his son, Davey Ray Nolan.*

58

That night, Red Thallon stood outside the Broken Spoke on South Lamar in denim cut off shorts and bedazzled cowboy boots with her microphone in hand. Austin musicians, politicians, and friends of Merit and her staff filed into the doors of the night spot.

Red got the countdown from her cameraman and began.

"We are here outside Austin's world famous honky-tonk and dance hall to celebrate the life of Liam Nolan. This long overdue tribute to one of our own comes at the end of a convoluted and dangerous probate fight resulting in loss of life for both Liam and his son Davey. Our heroine in this story is Merit Bridges and her staff who never gave up the fight to clear their clients' names and preserve the legacy that was expressly desired by both. You've heard a lot about Merit Bridges over the past few months. Let me be the final word in telling you that none of it was true. L.A. Baron not only hacked the mail and phone of Merit Bridges and her staff, he planted fake news to sully her reputation and incite litigation against her," Red said.

"A bitter campaign was waged by L.A. Baron, a famous music executive who has been found legally insane and is incarcerated in Austin State Hospital. Not since the 2016 election have we seen such an orchestrated attack on someone's character, reputation, and livelihood. Tonight, the victor is Merit Bridges. She celebrates here with Austin music lovers and her unwavering supporters. For the full story, go to Austin9Online. For now, let's two-step!"

Red killed the camera with a gesture to the throat, gave the cameraman her microphone, and went into the Broken Spoke to join the fun.

♪

Merit worked the crowd around the dance floor at the Broken Spoke. She wore a white blouse and a long denim skirt with handkerchief hem and a pair of black cowboy boots with white stitching. Her arms and neck were decorated with layers of silver and turquoise from her many trips to Santa Fe and Austin jewelry shops.

The bar was filled with her staff, clients, the new mayoral candidate and his entourage, and musicians from all over Austin. Hayes Carll, Alejandro Escobedo, and Ray Benson chatted in one corner.

She hugged Betty, Val, and Gilbert in turn. She swapped air kisses with her best friend Joy and her husband Tucker. They had driven Ace up from Houston for the celebration.

Merit held onto Ace's hand as she hugged Kim Wan and his wife, Clover.

"This never would have happened without your husband," Merit said.

Kim Wan beamed with pride.

Mayor Turner had not been invited and was not present, but City Councilman Burke Lee was there to represent. It was rumored he was going to challenge Turner in the next election and that Merit was supporting his candidacy. This time the news was true.

She shook hands with the new mayoral front runner.

"This is my son Ace," Merit said.

The candidate shook hands with Ace and presented a tiny blue eyed blond girl about twelve years old.

"This is my daughter, Ariel."

"Want to dance?" Ace asked.

She nodded and they twirled away across the dance floor.

Merit turned around and found herself facing Bo from Killer Delight. He held out a glass of wine.

"I think this has your name on it. Are you going to pour it out like last time?" Bo asked.

"I didn't know you saw that. I thought you were trying to poison me," Merit laughed.

"I was trying to ask you out until your son walked up," Harding said.

"In spite of all the gossip that was going around?" Merit asked.

"I never listen to that stuff. I just wanted to get you alone," Bo said.

"So, music talk with Ace won out?" Merit laughed.

"At least that night," Harding winked.

Ag looked over at Merit and rolled his eyes.

"Some things never change," Ag said to Betty.

Killer Delight went back onstage and Bo strapped on his guitar.

Merit thanked a few more guests then looked around the room and found her target. She stepped up behind Ag and tapped him on the shoulder.

"Dance?" Merit asked.

Ag turned around, looked surprised, then grinned his charming grin.

"Yes, ma'am."

Ace and Betty watched and smiled at each other.

Killer Delight's music filled the room with a cover of the Dixie Chick's *Some Days You Gotta' Dance*! Ag gave Merit a twirl then scooped her into his arms.

"I'm back," Merit said.

About the Author

Manning Wolfe, an author and attorney residing in Austin, Texas, writes cinematic-style, smart, fast-paced thrillers with a salting of Texas bullshit. The first in her series, featuring Austin Lawyer Merit Bridges, is Dollar Signs: Texas Lady Lawyer vs. Boots King. A graduate of Rice University and the University of Texas School of Law, Manning's experience has given her a voyeur's peek into some shady characters' lives and a front row seat to watch the good people who stand against them.

www.ManningWolfe.com

FOLLOW THE TEXAS LADY LAWYER GANG AND RECEIVE A FREE GIFT!

If you enjoyed Merit, Betty, Ag, and the whole Texas Lady Lawyer Gang, get notifications of their adventures and receive a free gift here:

http://manningwolfe.com/free-cookbook/

You will also be notified of contests, drawings, and giveaways of free Kindles, Gift Cards, and Texas Lady Lawyer souvenirs.

If you enjoyed this book, please leave a REVIEW on Amazon or Goodreads. Reviews are the lifeblood of authors and often determine whether other readers purchase books when they shop. Thank you. www.manningwolfe.com